Adventures in

Sherlockian Aesthetic Realism:

Sherlock Holmes Cartoons

from a warped mind

Volume 3

By

Don Hobbs

Paperback ISBN 978-1-78705-862-0

Published by MX Publishing
335 Princess Park Manor, Royal Drive,
London, N11 3GX
www.mxpublishing.co.uk

Cover design by Brian Belanger

To

Peter E. Blau, raconteur extraordinaire, bottomless wealth of Sherlockian knowledge, and all around ambassador the Grand Game we play.

Contents

221 Sherlockian Aesthetic Realism drawings by Don Hobbs with a canonical explanation accompanying each.

Foreword

This all started in the fall of 2011 when my wife Joyce and I stumbled across the Napoleon Museum during our "Roaming Rome" vacation. Inside there was an art exhibit by Chiam Koppleman, the American artist known for his works of Aesthetic Realism. The exhibit was entitled 'Napoleon Enters New York' and it featured drawings and paintings of Napoleon in various unfamiliar settings, like entering Coney Island or riding alligators. His Bicones hat and his epaulette-coat were always present in the pictures and something about this exhibit struck a chord with me. Immediately I knew I had to start my own series of drawings. Thus was born Aesthetic Sherlockian Realism. The pipe and deerstalker replace the epaulettes and Bicones. The Master replaces the Emperor. So enjoy my artistic adventure where the game is afoot.

Sherlock Holmes Goes Spelunking

"...the caveman to the angel..." ILLU

Sherlock Holmes Visits the Astrodome

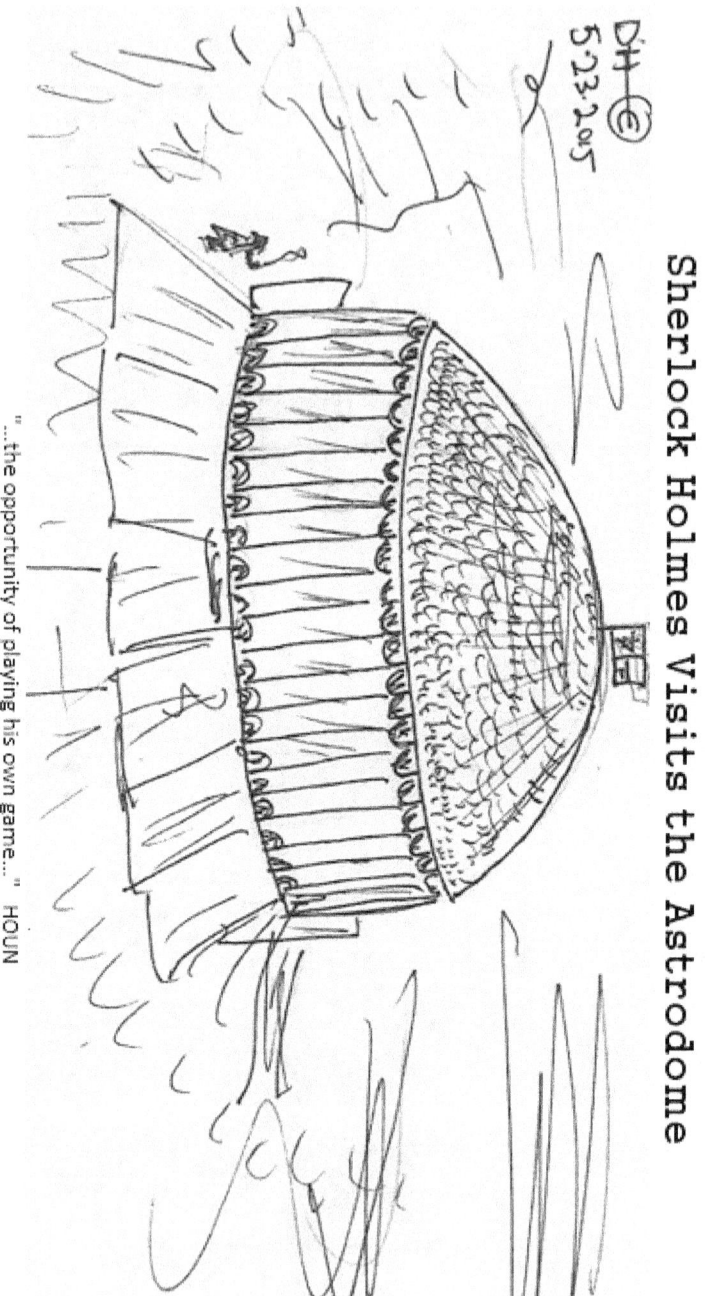

"...the opportunity of playing his own game..." HOUN

DH E
5·23·2005

Sherlock Holmes Likes Pegasus–Dallas

"...As to the missing horse, there are abundant proofs in the mud..." SILV

3

"...well, here's to your good health, landlord, and property to your house..." BLUE

4

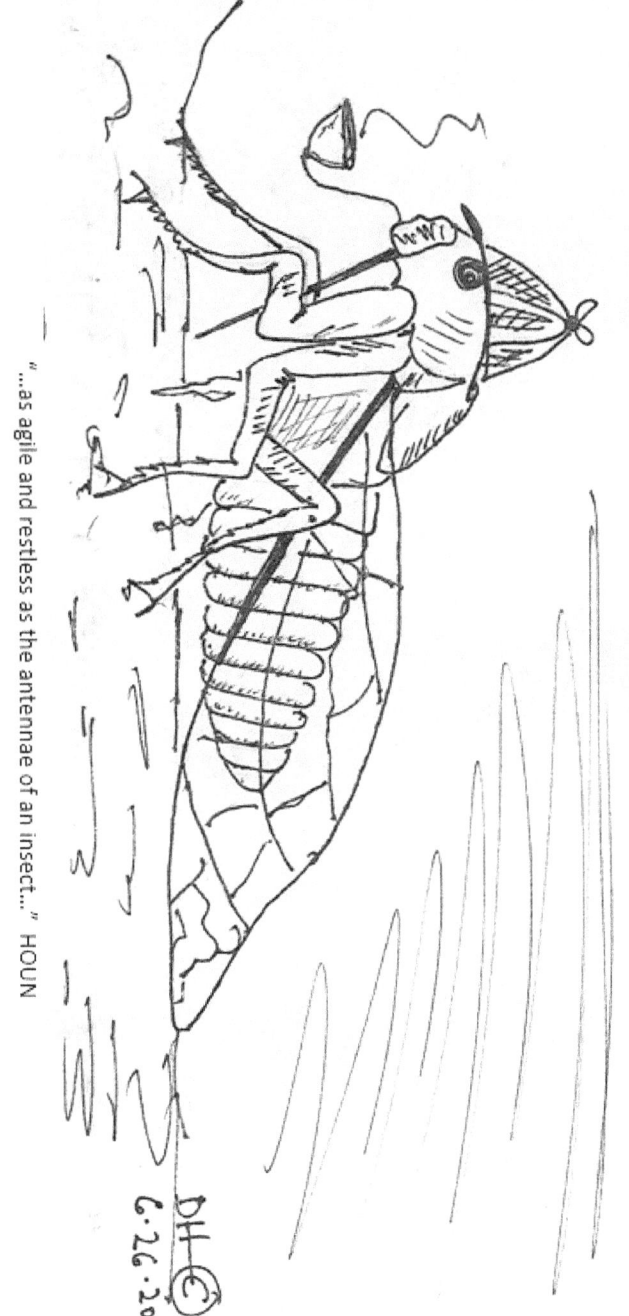

Sherlock Holmes Loves Cicadas

"...as agile and restless as the antennae of an insect..." HOUN

DH
6·26·2015

5

Sherlock Holmes Enjoys the World Cup

"... Oxford won by a goal and two tries..." MISS

Sherlock Holmes Chasing a Butterfly

DH
10·5·2015

"...and he carried a green butterfly net..." HOUN

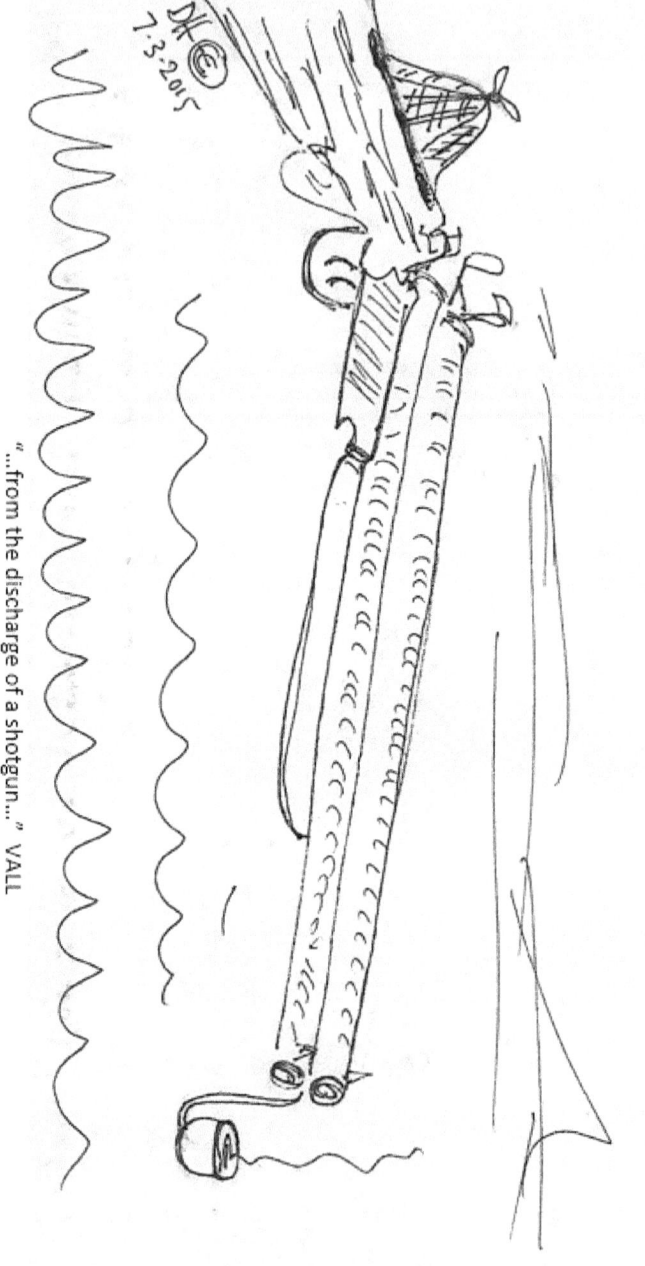

Sherlock Holmes and His 410 Shotgun

"...from the discharge of a shotgun..." VALL

DH
7-3-2015

8

Sherlock Holmes Has a Fortune Cookie

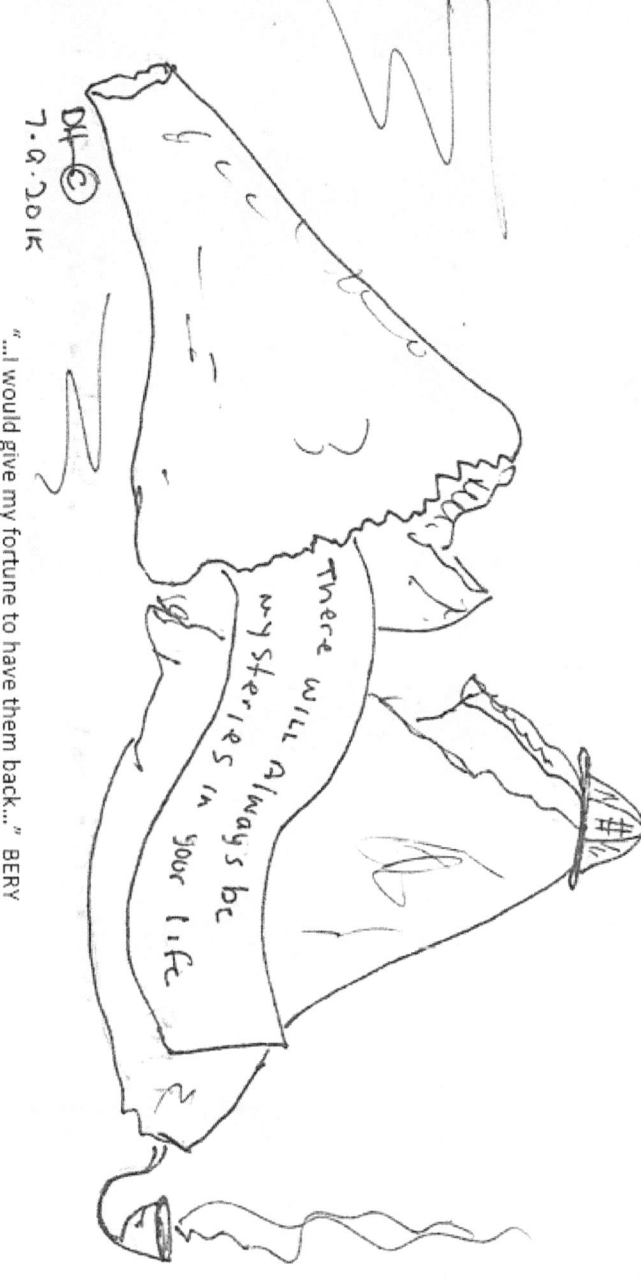

"...I would give my fortune to have them back..." BERY

DH-C
7·9·2018

There will Always be mysteries in your life

Sherlock Holmes Loathes the Stars and Bars

"...A confederate who foresees your conclusions and course of action is always dangerous..." BLAN

DH-C. 7.2.2015

Sherlock Holmes Has a Randy's Donut

"...and I'll manage to send him a message letting him know the hole we are in..." STUD

"...any articles which afford a finer field..." GOLD

"...what it was that give him that senile and decrepit appearance..." STUD

Sherlock Holmes Dreams He Can Fly

" ... I find it hard enough to tackle facts, Holmes, without flying away after theories and fantasies.... "   BOSC

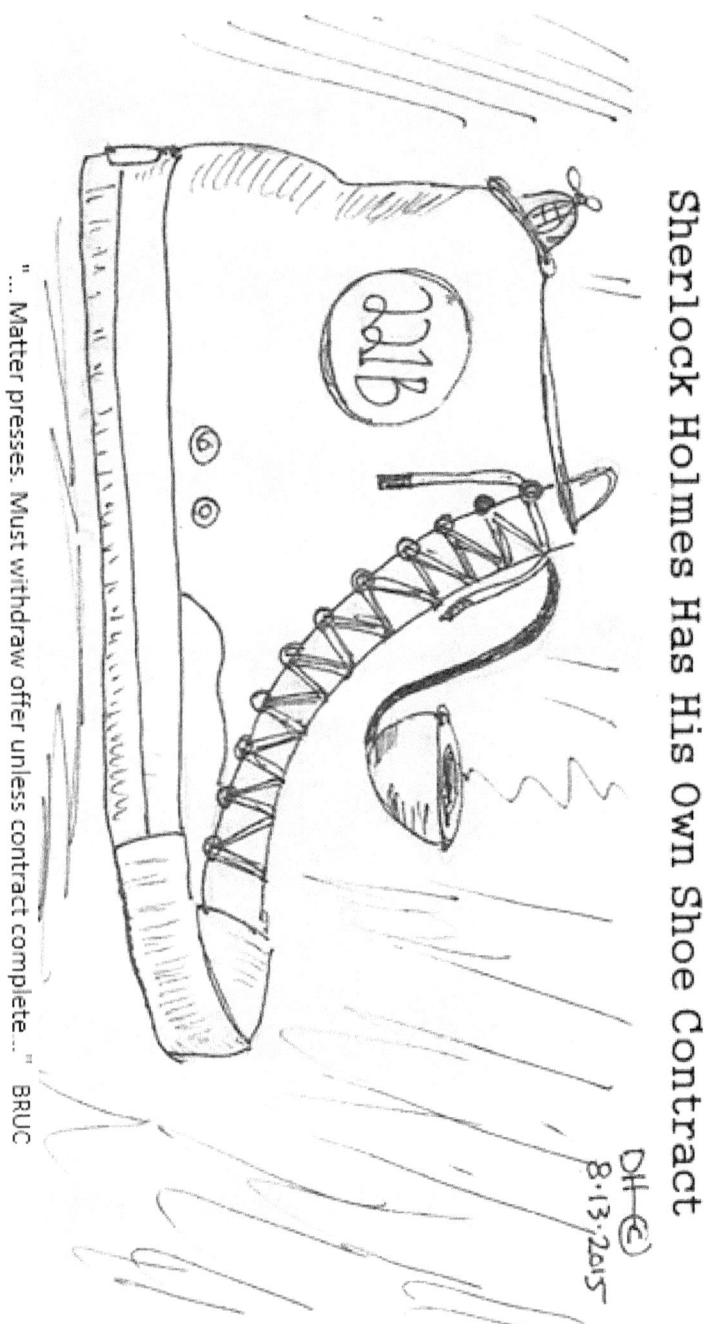

Sherlock Holmes Has His Own Shoe Contract

"... Matter presses. Must withdraw offer unless contract complete..." BRUC

DH-©
8·13·2015

Sherlock Holmes Pilots a Whirlybird

"...In the whirl of our incessent activities..." SOLI

16

Sherlock Holmes Lives on a Yellow Submarine

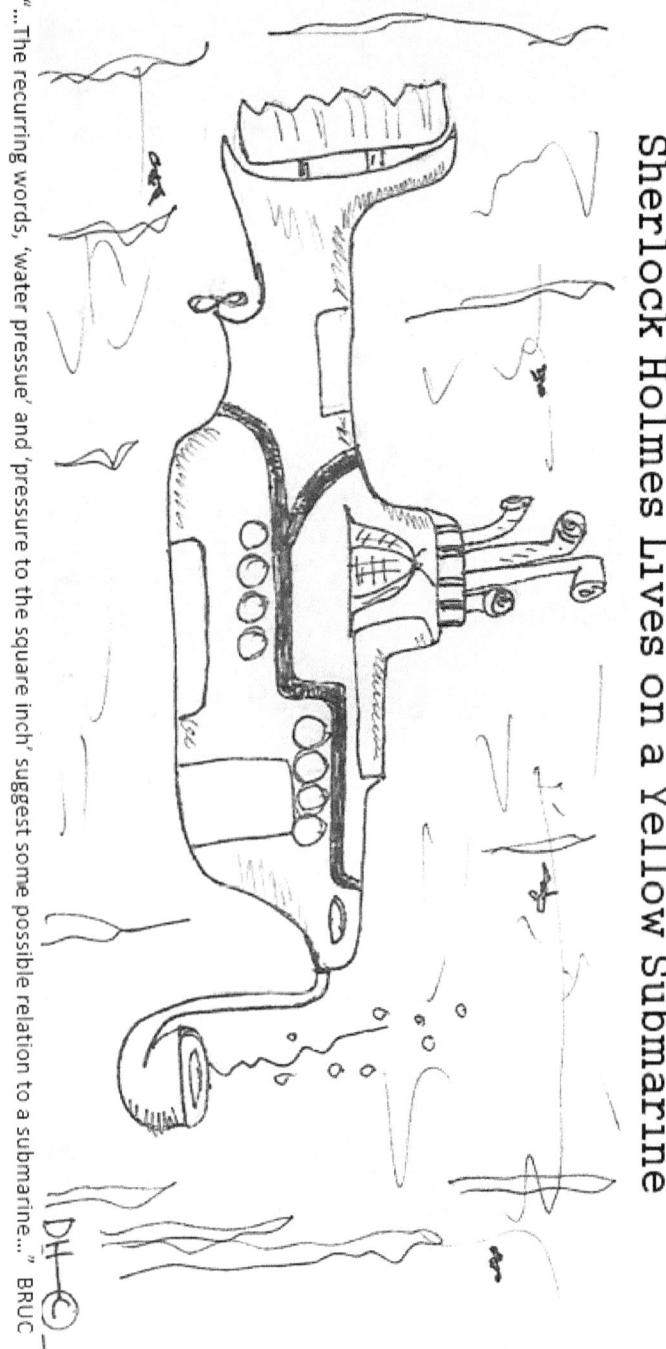

"...The recurring words, 'water pressure' and 'pressure to the square inch' suggest some possible relation to a submarine..." BRUC

Sherlock Holmes Plays a Banjo

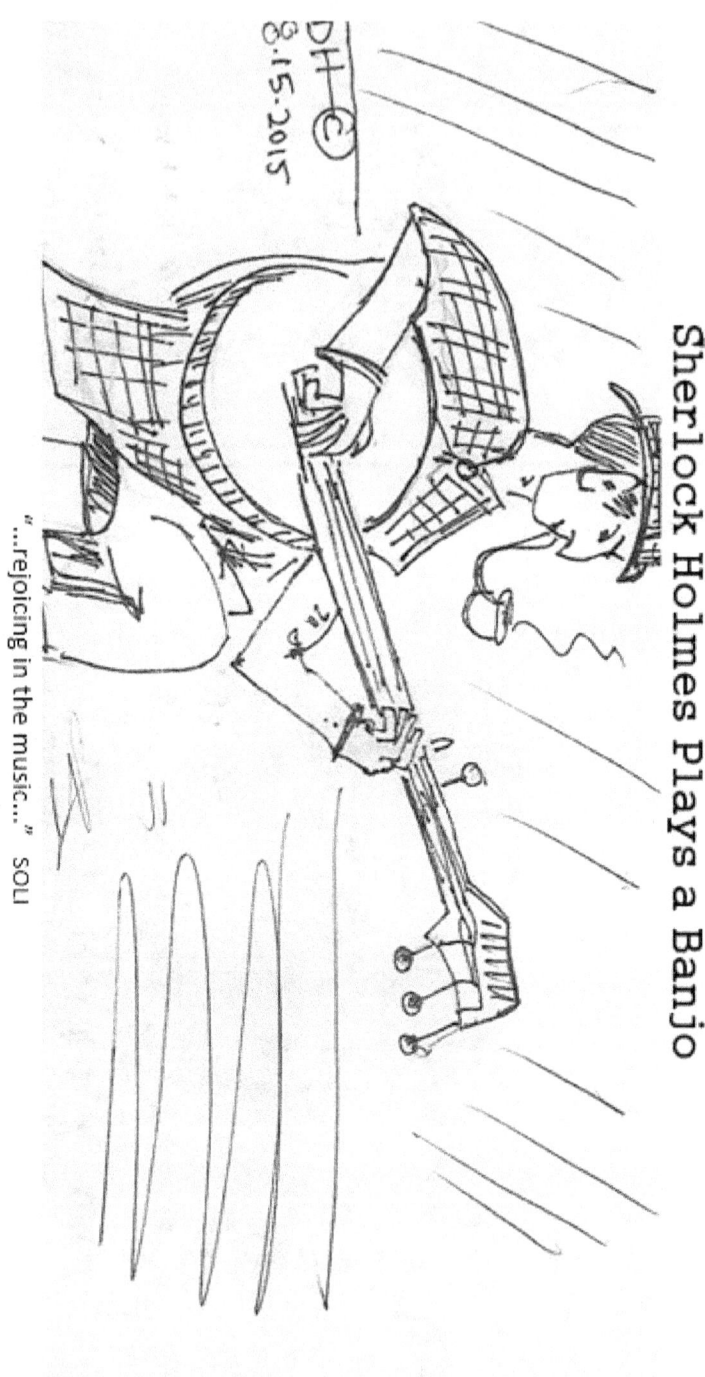

"...rejoicing in the music...." SOLI

18

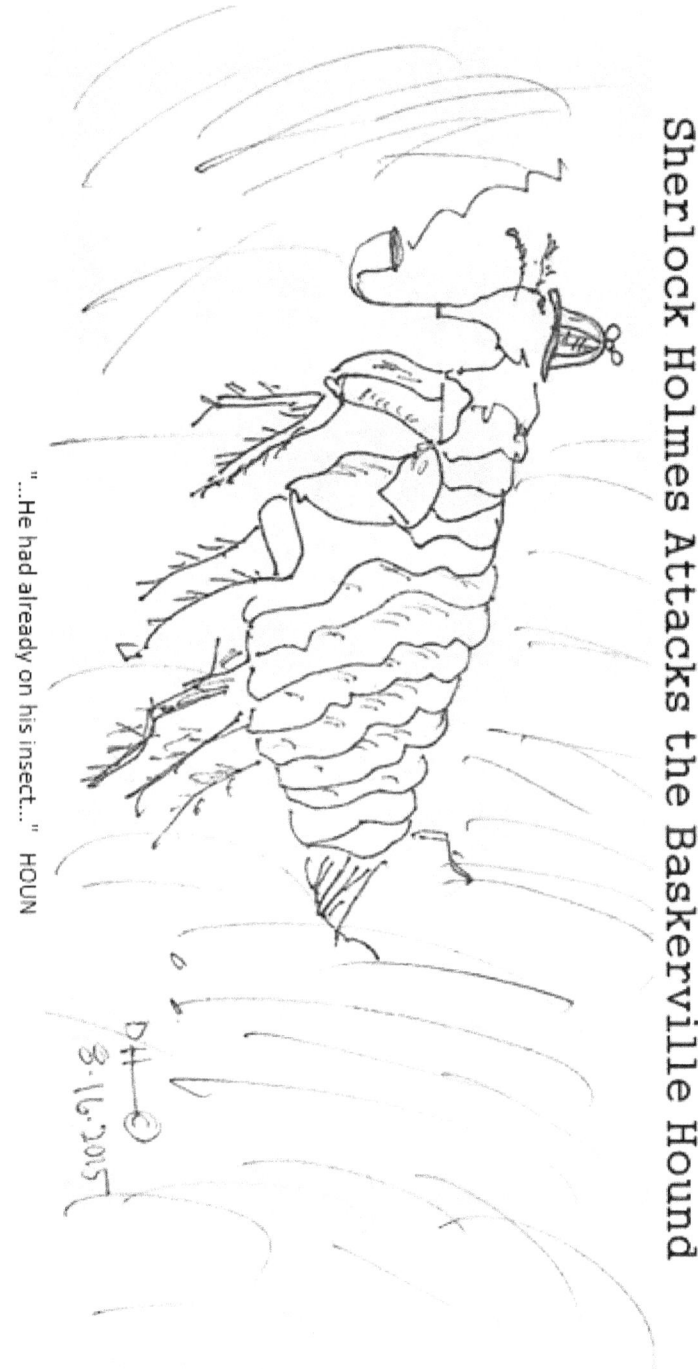

Sherlock Holmes Attacks the Baskerville Hound

"...He had already on his insect..." HOUN

19

Sherlock Holmes is Never Squirrelly

"...six foot three in height, active as a squirrel..." ABBE

Sherlock Holmes Disguised as a Dragonfly

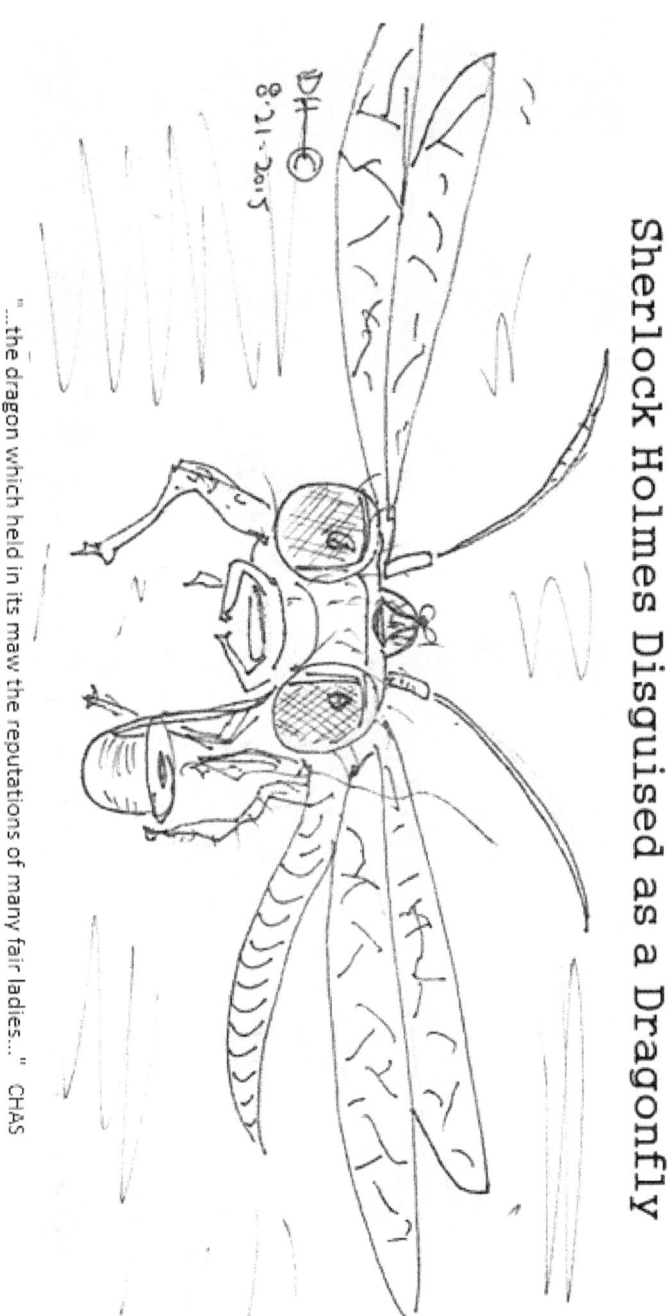

"...the dragon which held in its maw the reputations of many fair ladies..." CHAS

Sherlock Holmes Uses Sky-Link at D.F.W.

"...scuttling across the sky..." CREE

22

Sherlock Holmes Cutting a Rug

"...we'd best put it back on the rug where we found it...." VALL

Sherlock Holmes Thinking of Napoleon

"...This Dr. Barnicot is an enthusiastic admirer of Napoleon..." SIXN

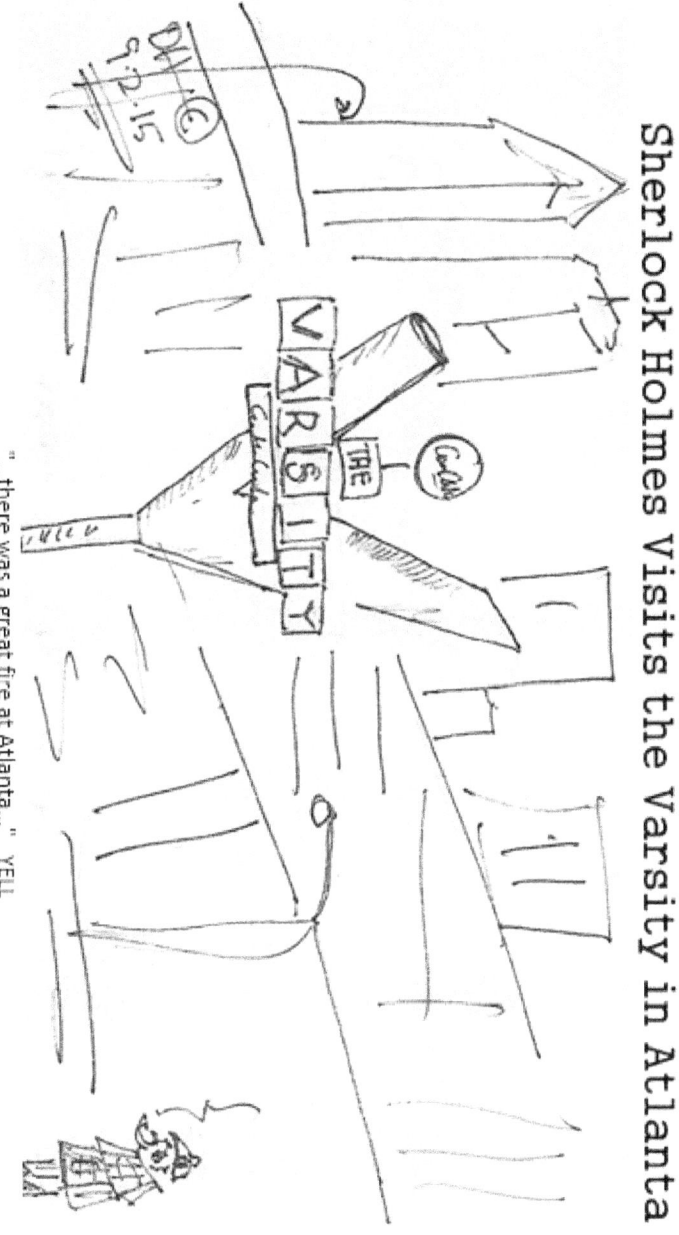

"...there was a great fire at Atlanta..." YELL

25

Sherlock Holmes: English Muffin

"...but this really tastes like cake..." TWIS

Sherlock Holmes Plays Opposum!!

"...She seemed half dead..." ABBE

Sherlock Holmes Loves His Pick–Up Truck

"...But I tell you now that if it is anything against the safety of the fort I will have no truck with it..."   SIGN

Sherlock Holmes Uses Apple

"...My dear fellow, he will guard it as the apple of his eye..." SILV

DH
9.19.15

29

Sherlock Holmes Rides the Merry—Go—Round

"...as the work was mostly to be done on horseback..." SIGN

Sherlock Holmes Cheerleader

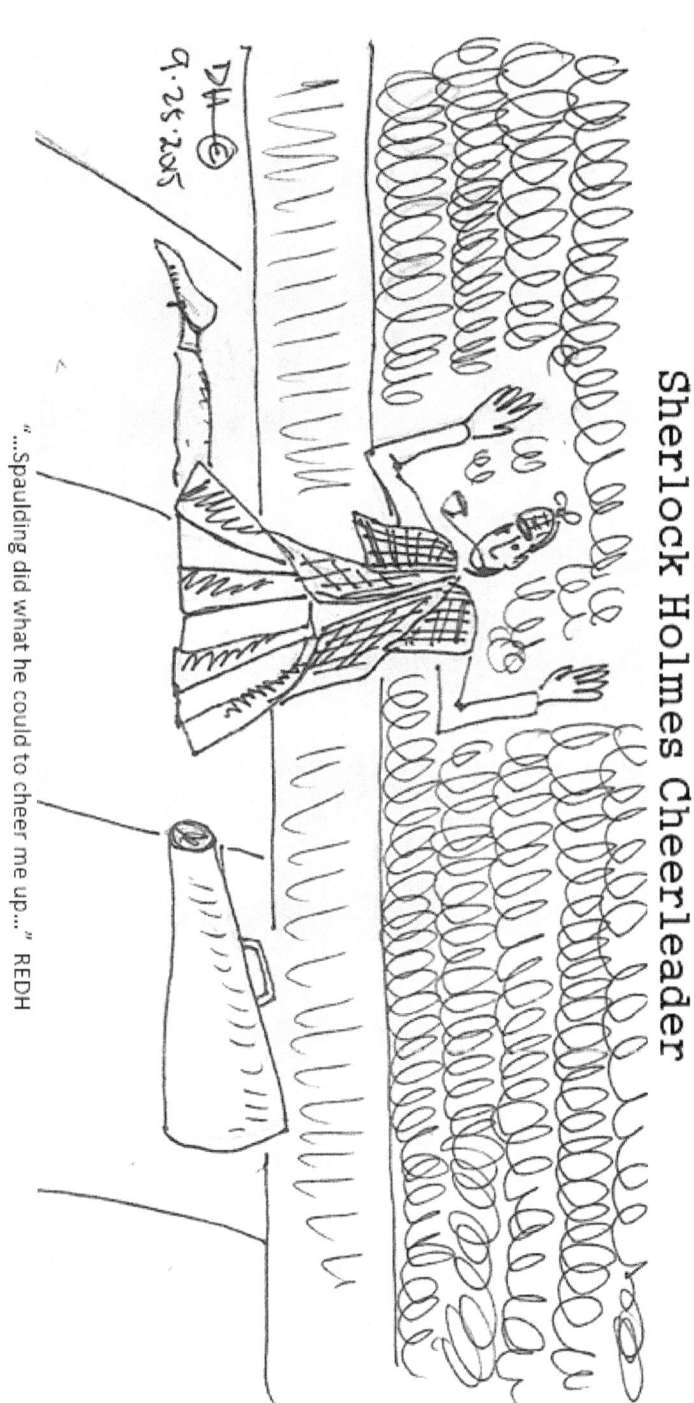

"...Spaulding did what he could to cheer me up..." REDH

Sherlock Holmes Yachtsman

"...It was their Rock of Gibralter, the largest and best boat..." ABBE

Sherlock Holmes Wants to Be a Pirate

"...The hoarse voice of the seaman broke in on our conversation..." BLAC

33

"...And yet it cannot be denied that the prosperity of the whole poor, bleak countryside depends on his presense..." EMPT

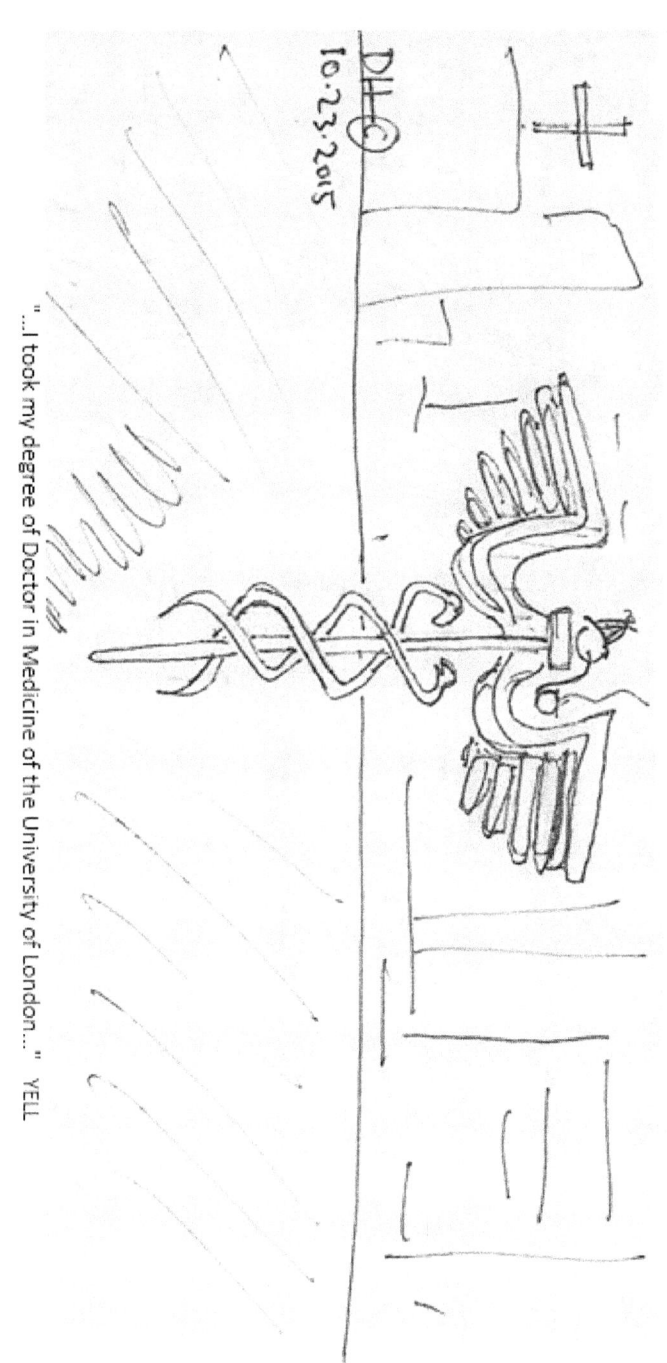

Sherlock Holmes Caduceus

DH (C)
10.23.2015

"...I took my degree of Doctor in Medicine of the University of London..."   YELL

35

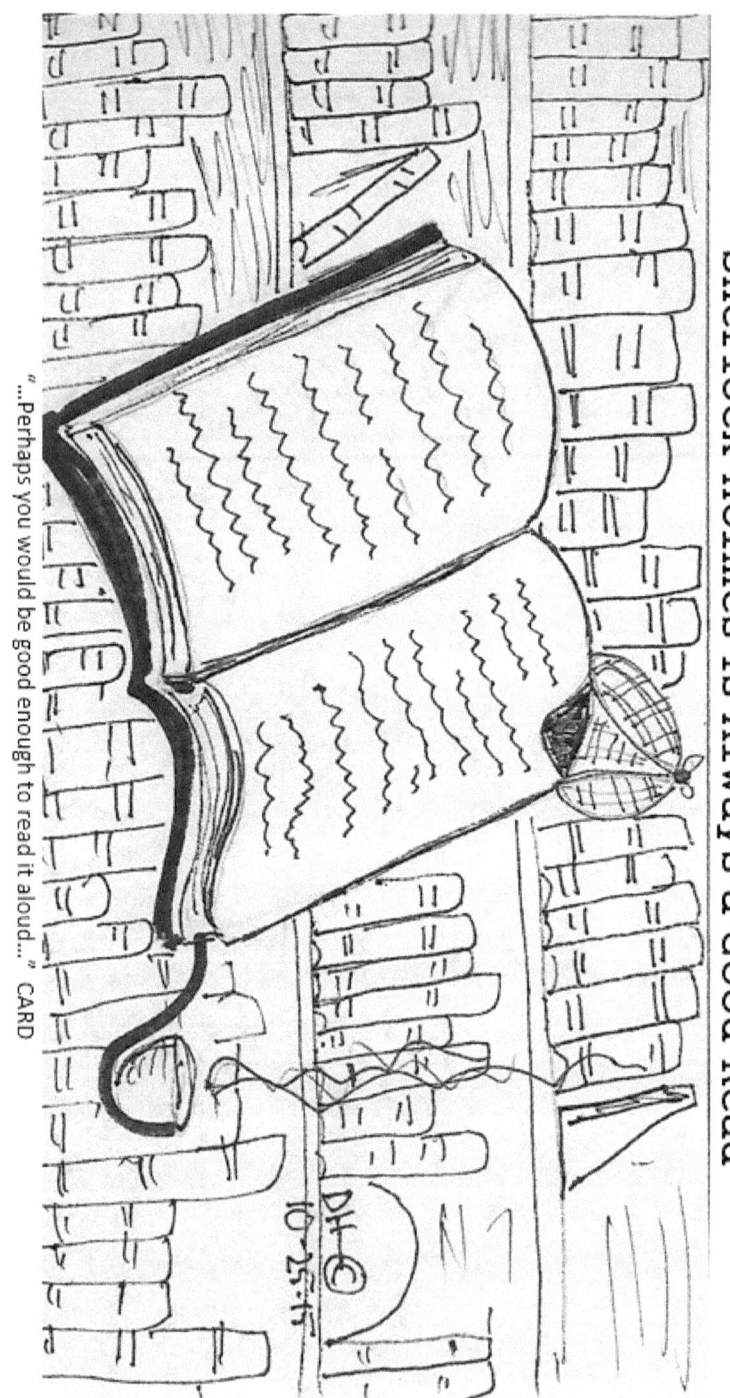

"...Perhaps you would be good enough to read it aloud..." CARD

Sherlock Holmes Loves Griffins

"...many of them adorned with griffin and coronet..." SHOS

Sherlock Holmes a Staple Kinda Guy

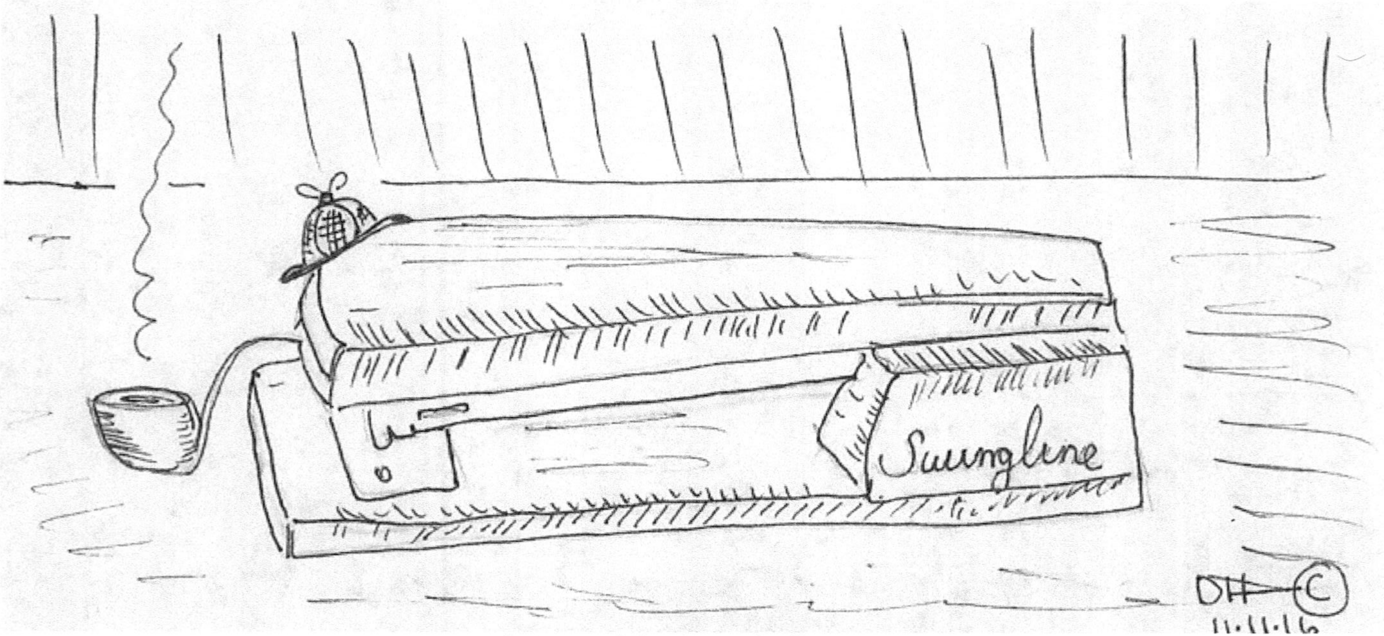

"...In one of these a staple..." HOUN

38

Sherlock Holmes Is Out of This World

"...To you they are like crimes committed in some other planet...." WIST

Sherlock Holmes Rides the Bus

GREYHOUND

"...so he took a bus home..." REDC

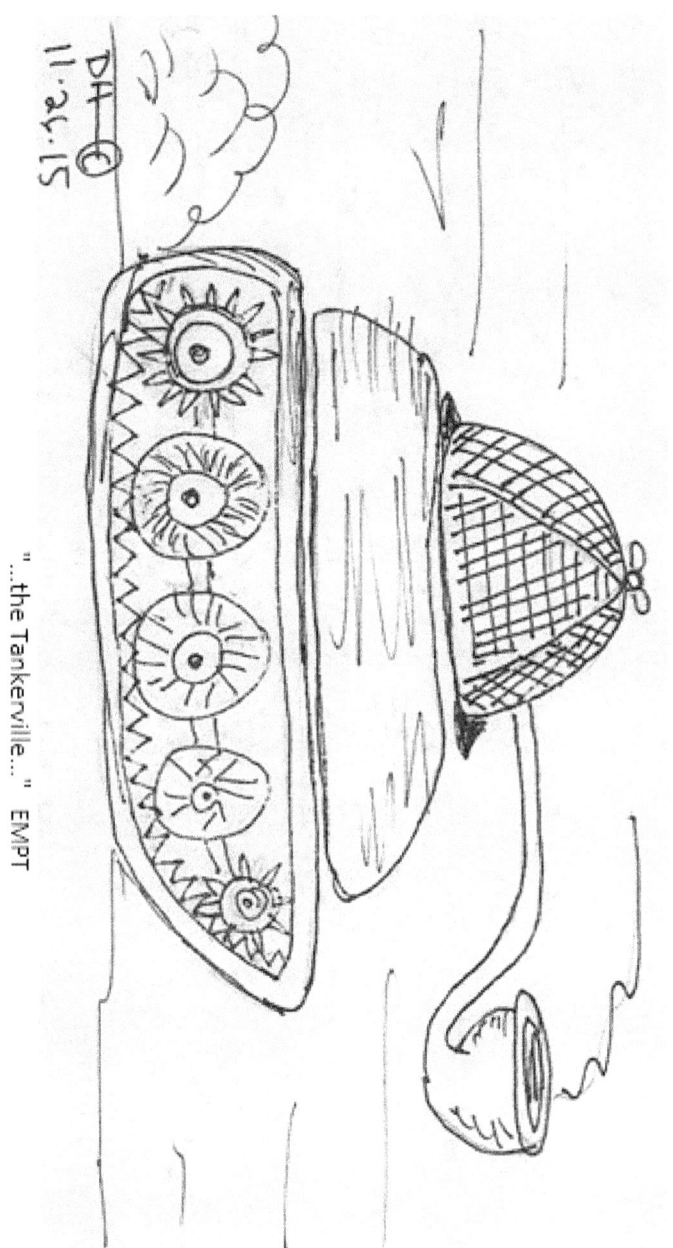

Sherlock Holmes Tank

"...the Tankerville..."   EMPT

DA
11.26.15

41

Sherlock Holmes Beekeeper

"...and my bees have the estate..." LION

42

Sherlock is Never Drifting

"...he saw the greasy, heavy, brown swirl still drifting past..." BRUC

Sherlock Holmes Sloth

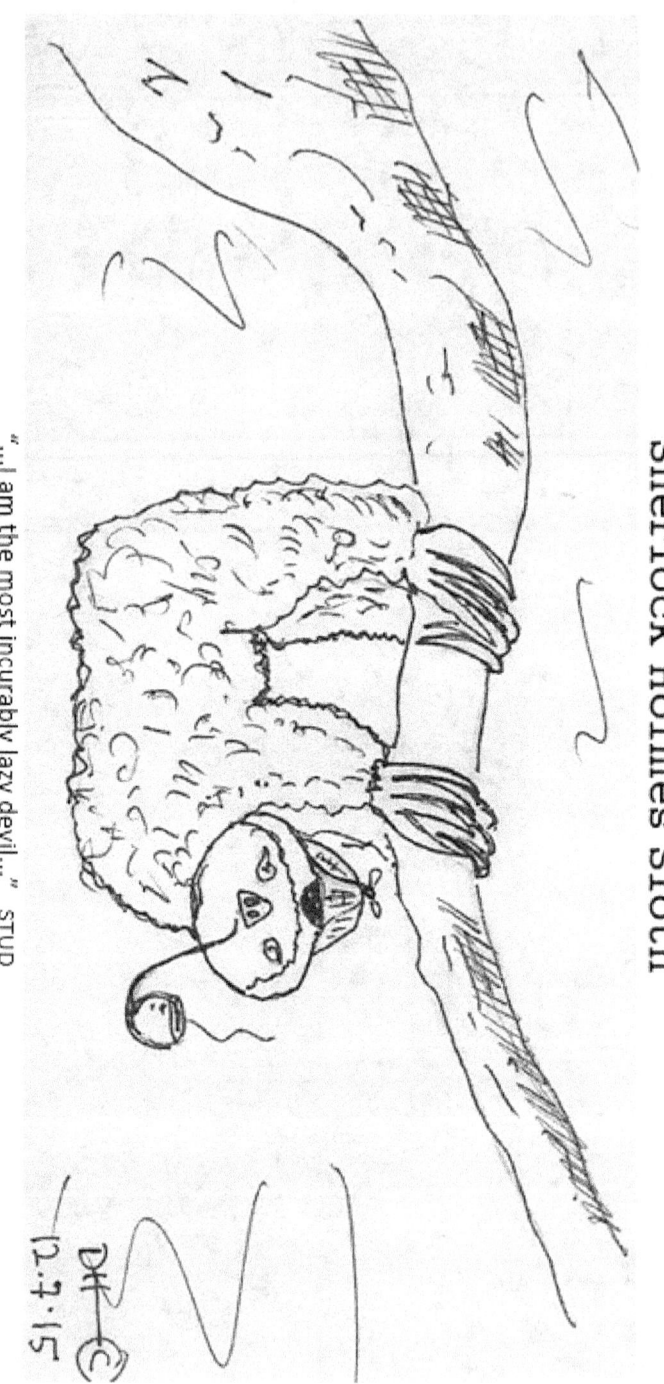

"...I am the most incurably lazy devil..." STUD

DH-C
12.7.15

Sherlock Holmes visits Mt. Kilomanjaro

"...in the districts of West Africa..." DEVI

45

Sherlock Holmes on the Mississippi

"...From the shores of the Mississippi to the western slopes of the Rocky Mountains..." STUD

46

Sherlock Holmes Plays Beach Volleyball

"...I came on little patches of sand..." LION

"...His hair and moustche were raven black...." ILLU

Sherlock Holmes Back at the Grand Canyon

"...and there was an abyss before him..." VALL

DH
9.3.2016
©

49

Sherlock Holmes in a Pram

"...Even when she was just a baby...." BOSC

DH-© 9.8.2016

Sherlock Holmes a Wild n Crazy Guy

"...You're crazy!" he cried..." DANC

Sherlock Holmes Rings a Bell – Montepulciano

" ...No one could possibly hear a bell ring ... "   ABBE

52

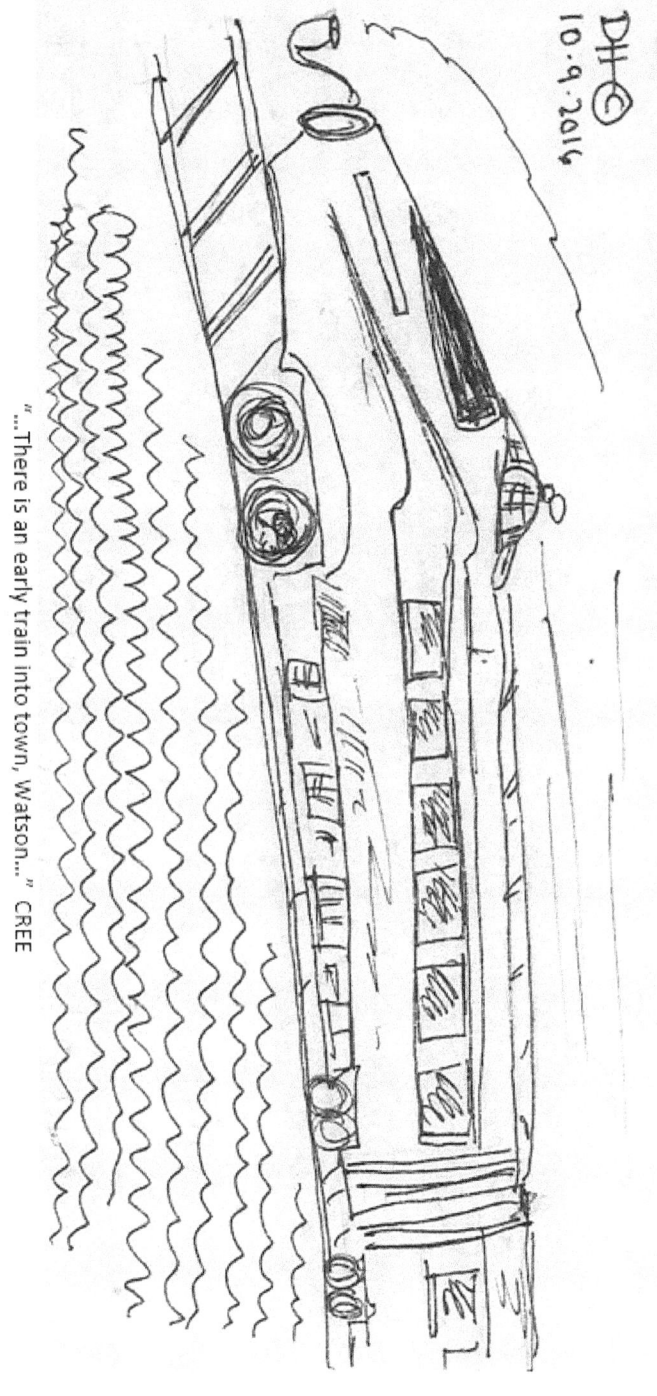

Sherlock Holmes Rides Trenitalia

"...There is an early train into town, Watson...." CREE

53

Sherlock Holmes Plays Jacks

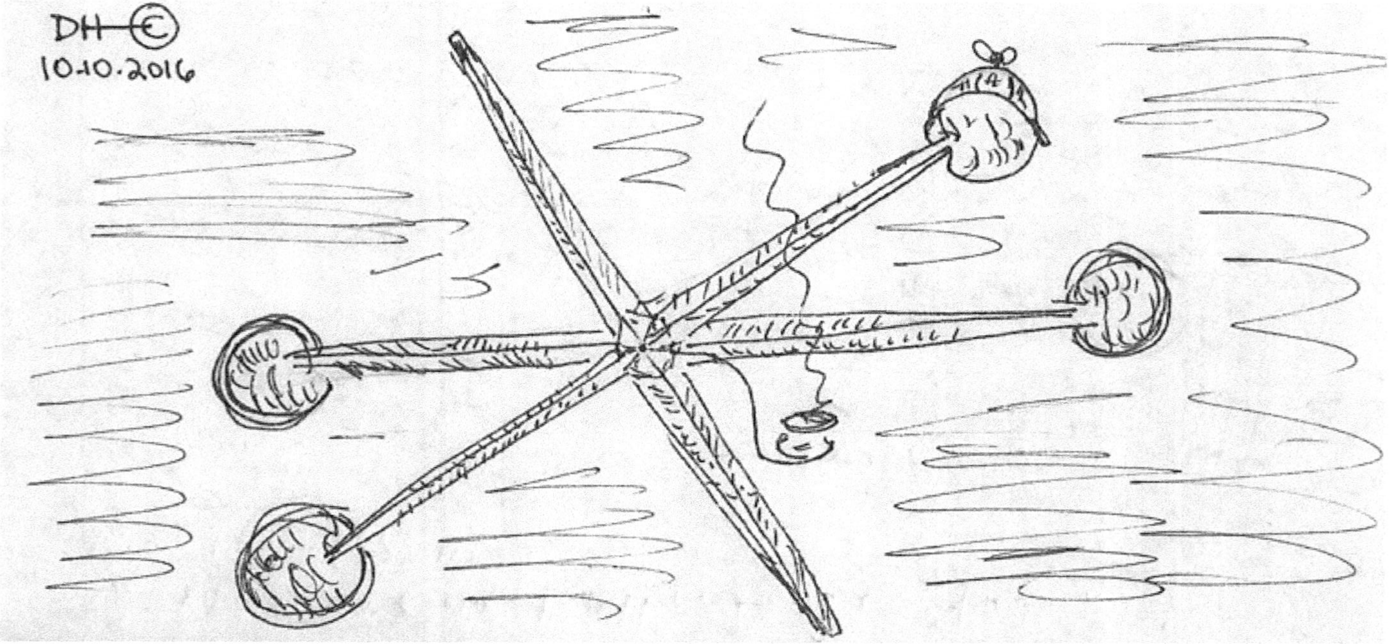

"...Black Jack of Ballart was the name I went under...." BOSC

DH © 10.10.2016

54

Sherlock Holmes Ganesha

"...From India..." FIVE

55

Sherlock Holmes Putting Out the Library Fire

"...a small but select library...." GLOR

Sherlock Holmes Keeps on Triking

"...A Flour-Wheeler was brought, and we all three drove back..." NAVA

Sherlock Holmes on a Hover-Board

"...and hover over the great city...." IDEN

Sherlock Holmes Love Construction Cranes

"...Mr. Armitge, of Crane Water, near Reading...." SPEC

DH·C
9·17·11

59

Sherlock Holmes Mantis

"...she was a ready prey for any adventure..." RETI

DHC
11-17-16

Sherlock Holmes Doubles-Out

"...he came to leave his club, and some of his darts, too..." STUD

Sherlock Holmes Likes Each Band Equally

THE **BEATLES**

"...When you drove home after the concert I called upon Scotland Yard..." REDH

Sherlock Holmes Where the Buffalo Roam

"...Oh, How simple it would have been had I been here before they came in like a herd of buffalo..." BOSC

Sherlock Holmes Loves Triceratops

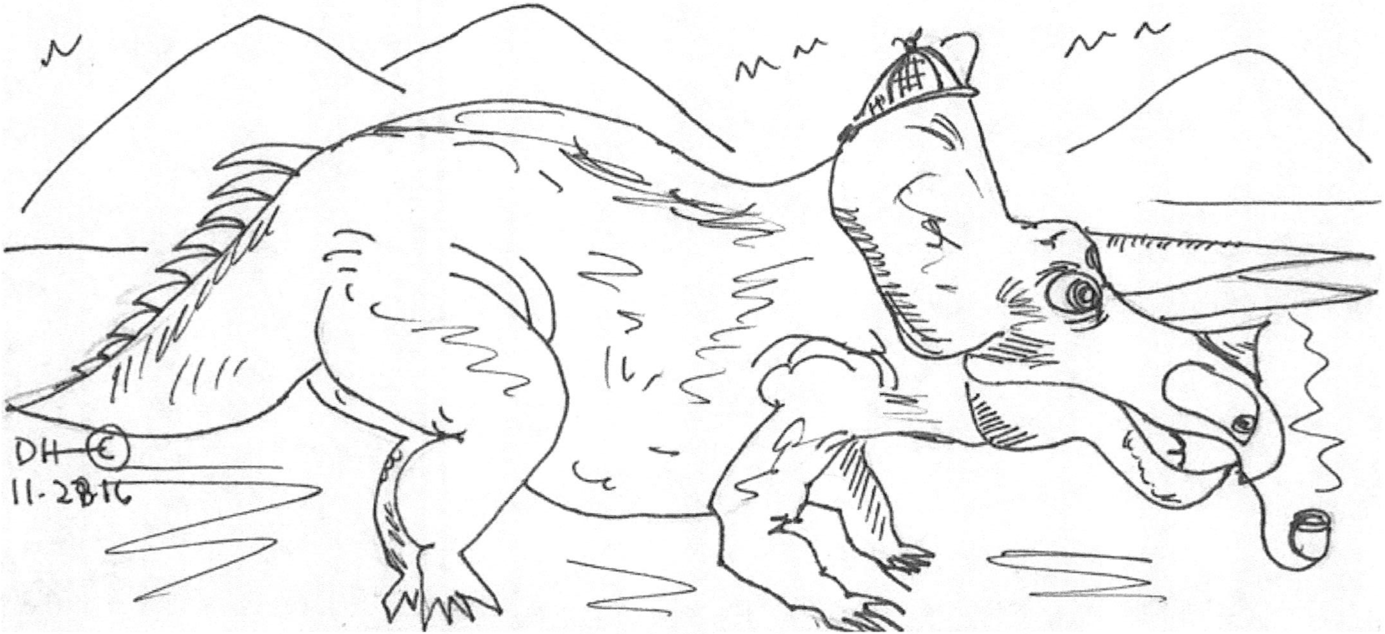

"...a prehistoric skull which fill him with great joy..." HOUN

Sherlock Holmes Drone

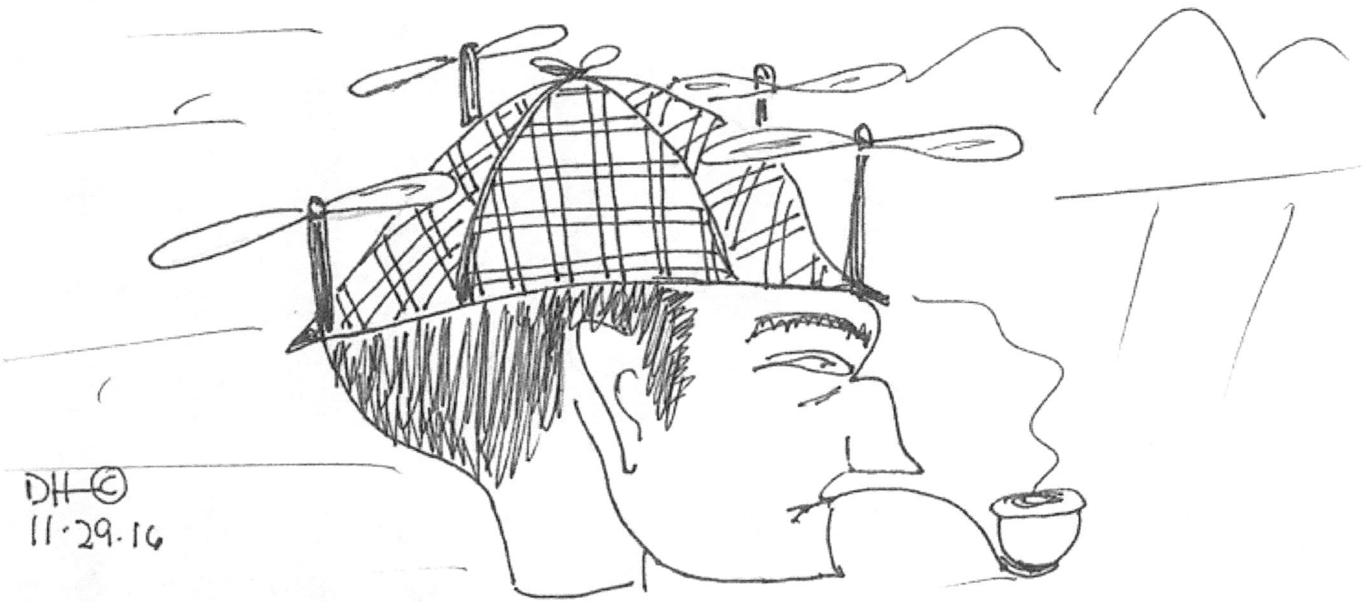

"....a kind of drone...." MISS

DH© 11·29·16

65

Sherlock Holmes Scorpion King

"...let him be aware, for this is a fearful stinger..." LION]

DHC
1·04·17

66

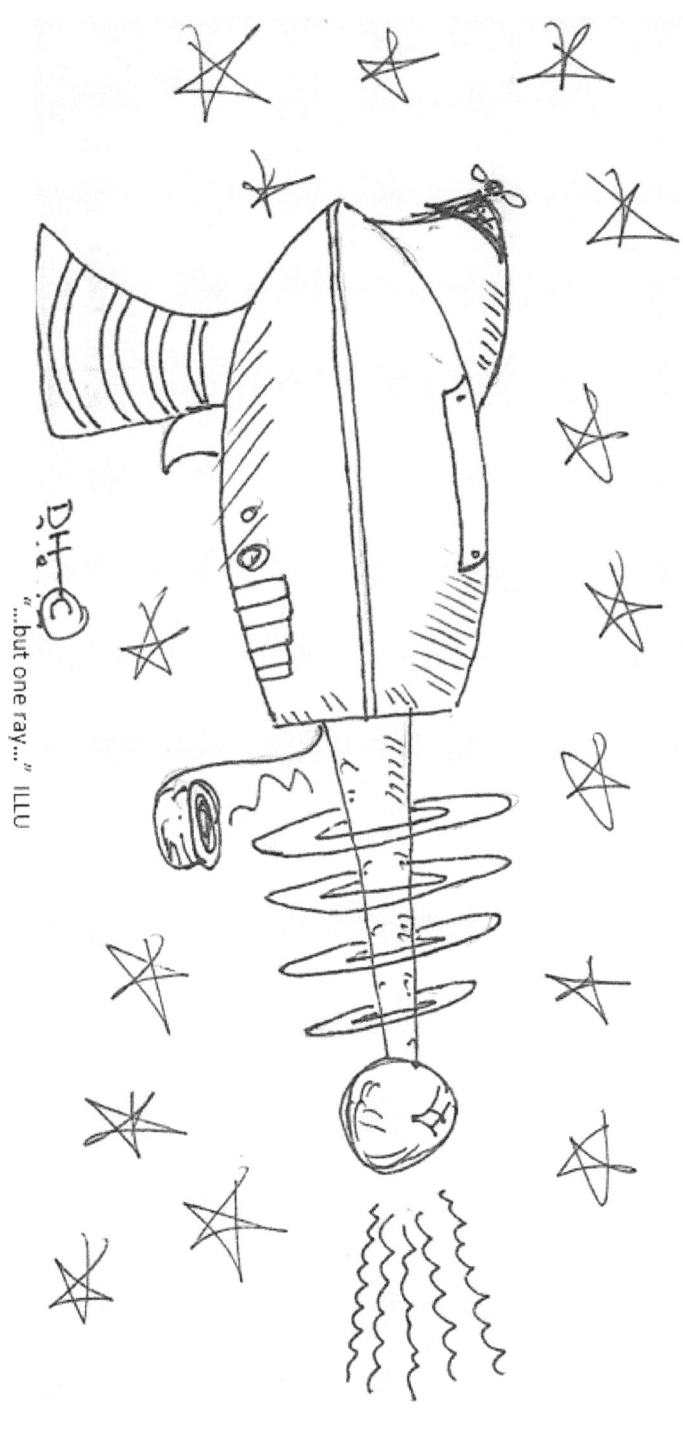

Sherlock Holmes Ray Gun

"...but one ray...." ILLU

Sherlock Holmes Is On TV

"...you may set your mind at rest..." BERY

Sherlock Holmes Phone Home

"...There is a private telephone call..." ILLU

DH-C
2.8.17

Sherlock Holmes Flies the Friendly Skies

"...that two middled aged gentlemen are flying westward..." BOSC

DH
2.18.17

Sherlock Holmes Is Still the Best

"...As it emerged into the moonshine I saw what it was..." COPP

Sherlock Holmes Pedal Car

"...caused by friction on the pedal..." SOLI

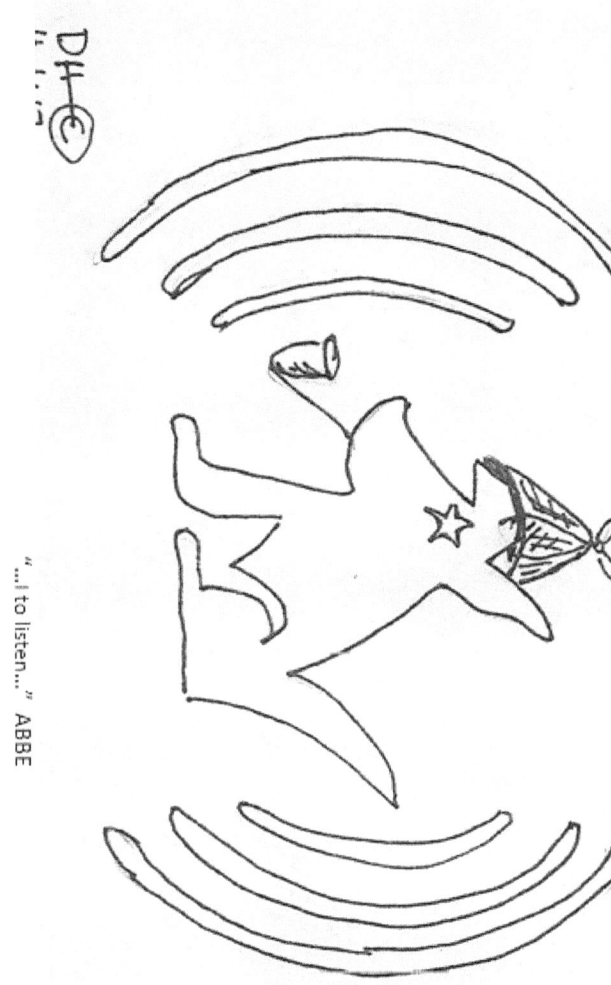

Sherlock Holmes Enjoys Sirius Radio

"...I to listen...." ABBE

Sherlock Holmes Plays the Masters

"...spasmostic fashion from golf..." GREE

74

Sherlock Holmes Is the United Way

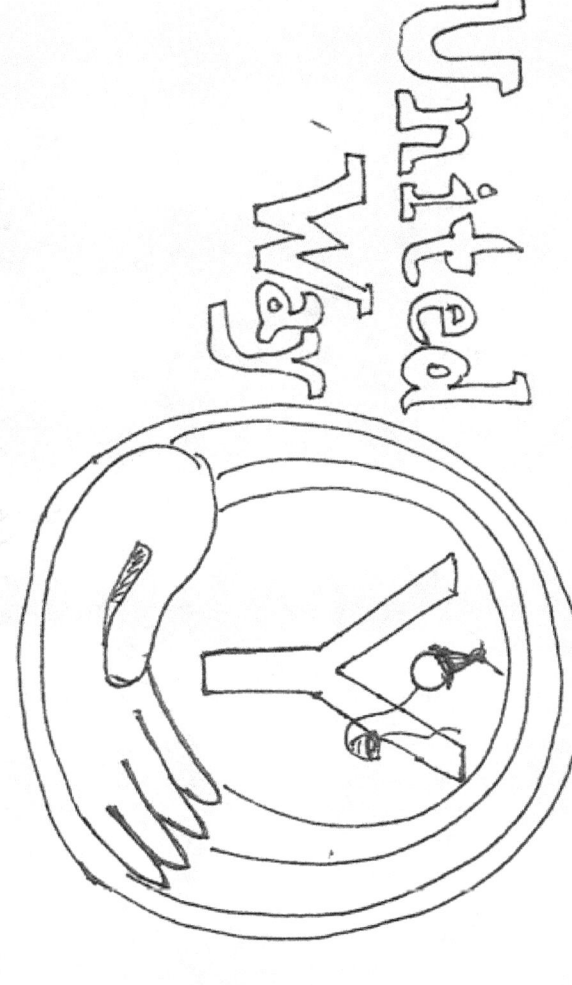

United Way

"...He had a reputation for kindness and charity..." GLOR

DH-C
4.12.13

75

Sherlock Holmes Always Rocks

"...It was the toy which he had promised to bring home..." CARD

DH©
4.10.17

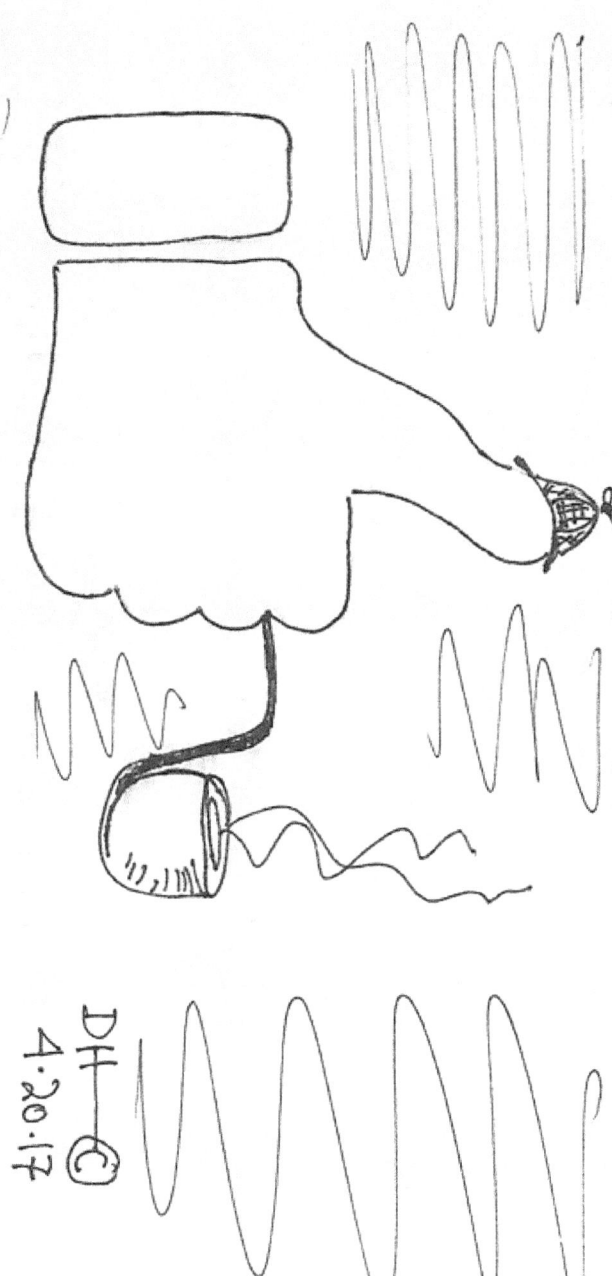

Sherlock Holmes Likes Facebook

"...It is unquestionably the mark of his thumb..." NORW

DH-©
4·20·17

77

"...What do you think of that, Watson?" cried Holmes in high glee, rubbing his hands together...." HOUN

78

Sherlock Holmes Visits Indy

"...He carries all our money for the race..." SHOS

79

Sherlock Holmes Gets Dental Implants

"...my companion had rambled about the room with his chin upon his chest and his brows knitted..."   SILV

Sherlock Holmes Is a Nikon Camera

"...snapping away with a camera..." REDH

DH
5·28·17

Sherlock Holmes Honors Memorial Day

Pay Respect

" ...a gallant verteran... " CROO

DHC
5·29·17

82

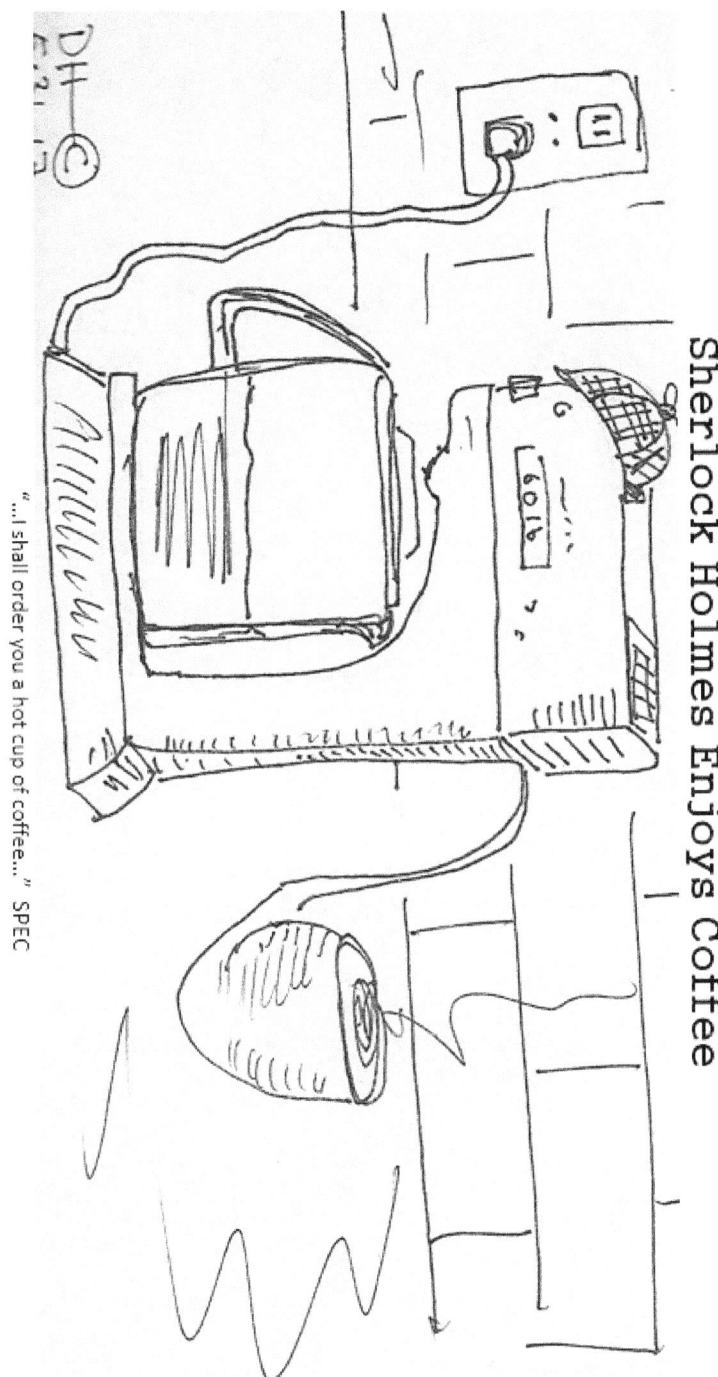

Sherlock Holmes Enjoys Coffee

"...I shall order you a hot cup of coffee..." SPEC

Sherlock Holmes Foots the Bill

"...For this purpose he pays large checks..." NORW

DH 5.31.17

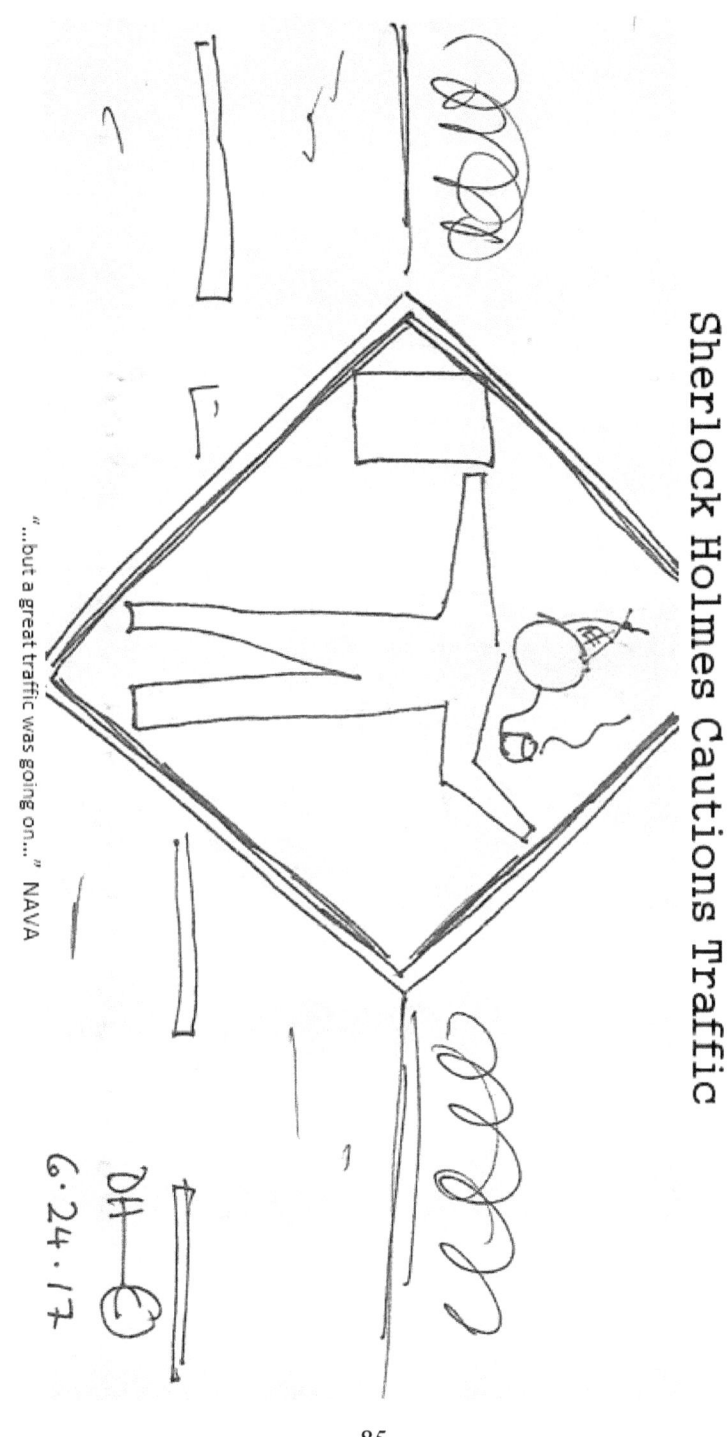

Sherlock Holmes Cautions Traffic

"...but a great traffic was going on..." NAVA

DH—6·24·17

85

Sherlock Holmes Loves July 4th

"...and it was July..." ABBE

DH©
7.4.17

"...My collection of M's is a fine one..." EMPT

DH—©
7.8.17

Sherlock Holmes Visits Dover

"...Let us walk the cliffs together..." DEVI

DHC
7.9.17

Sherlock Holmes Disguised as Jabba the Hut

"...a remarkable worm said to be unknown to science..." THOR

DH©
7·16·17

Sherlock Holmes Stuck Inside a Bottle

H.M.S. SHERLOCK

"...Yes, and the bottle stands as we left it..." ABBE

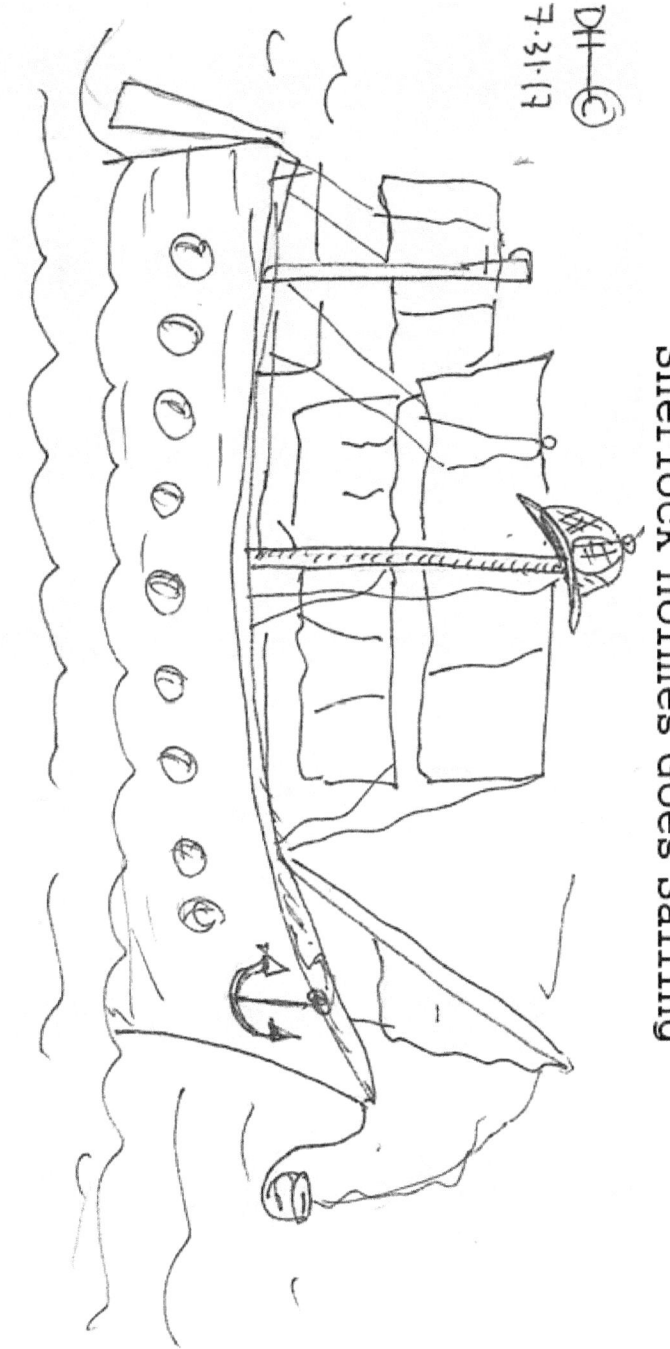

Sherlock Holmes Goes Sailing

"...All seems plain sailing..." RETI

DH—© 7·31·17

"...You don't believe such nonsense as that?..." HOUN

Sherlock Holmes visits Ayer's Rock

"...One of the most unscrupulous rascals Australia has ever produced..." LADY

Sherlock Holmes Loves the Original
Dallas Cowboys Logo

"...some time as they brand cattle..." VALL

94

Sherlock Holmes Hurricane Watch

"...It has been pouring rain and blowing a hurricane ever since..." GOLD

Sherlock Holmes Gets Everyone's Goat

"...like a sheep..." FIVE

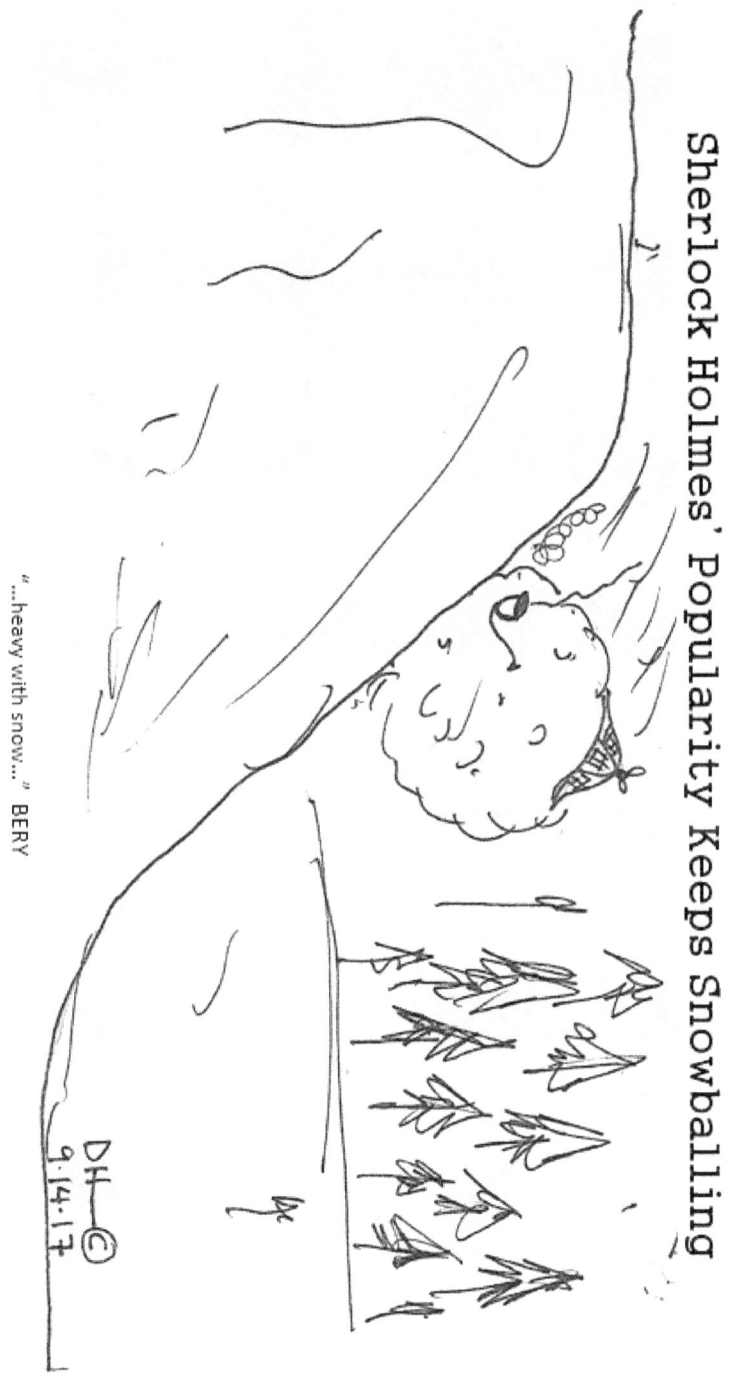

Sherlock Holmes' Popularity Keeps Snowballing

"...heavy with snow...." BERY

97

Sherlock Holmes Could Be an Ugly Fish

"...you will see a large and ugly gentleman...." MAZA

Sherlock Holmes Waves Good–Bye

"...I can remember the night when he bade farewell..." BLAC

Sherlock Holmes Practices the Piano

"...Next door there appeared to be a children's party for the merry buzz of young voices and the clatter of a piano resounded...." BRUC

Sherlock Holmes Is a Wise Old Bird

"...before the melancoly hooting of a mountain owl..." STUD

DH—C
10·6·17

Sherlock Holmes Fans Are Everywhere

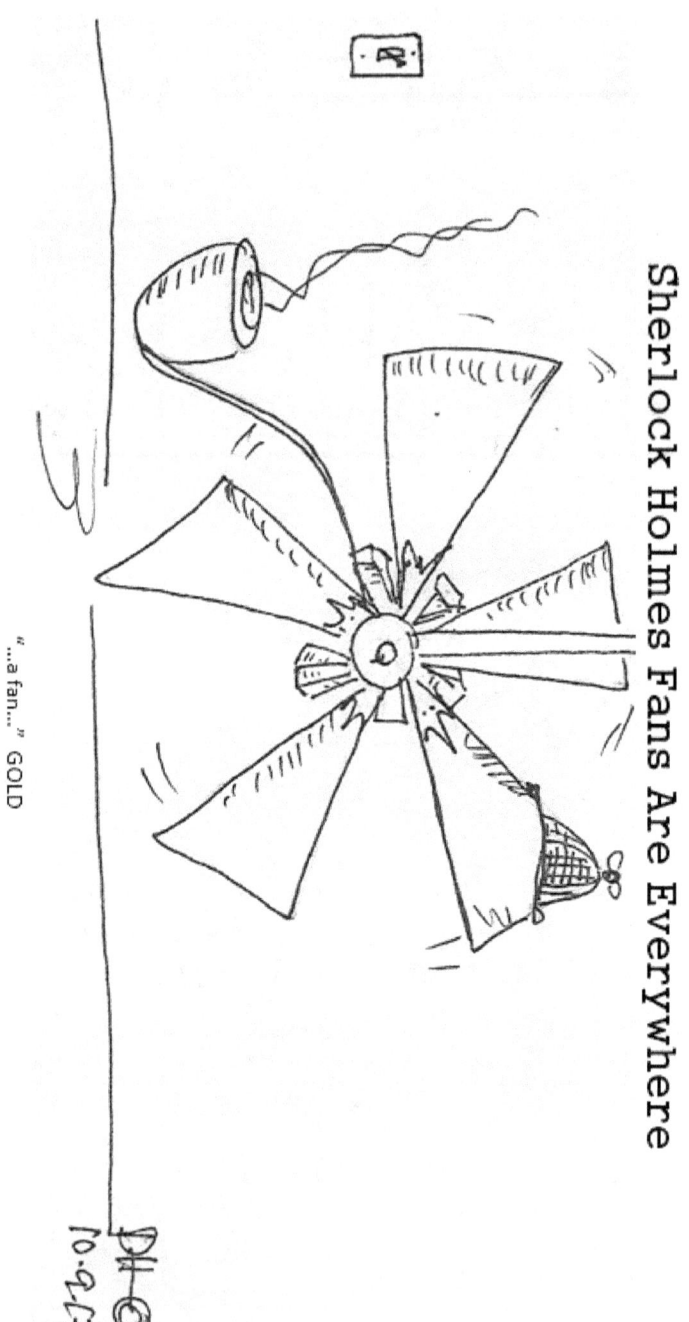

"...a fan...." GOLD

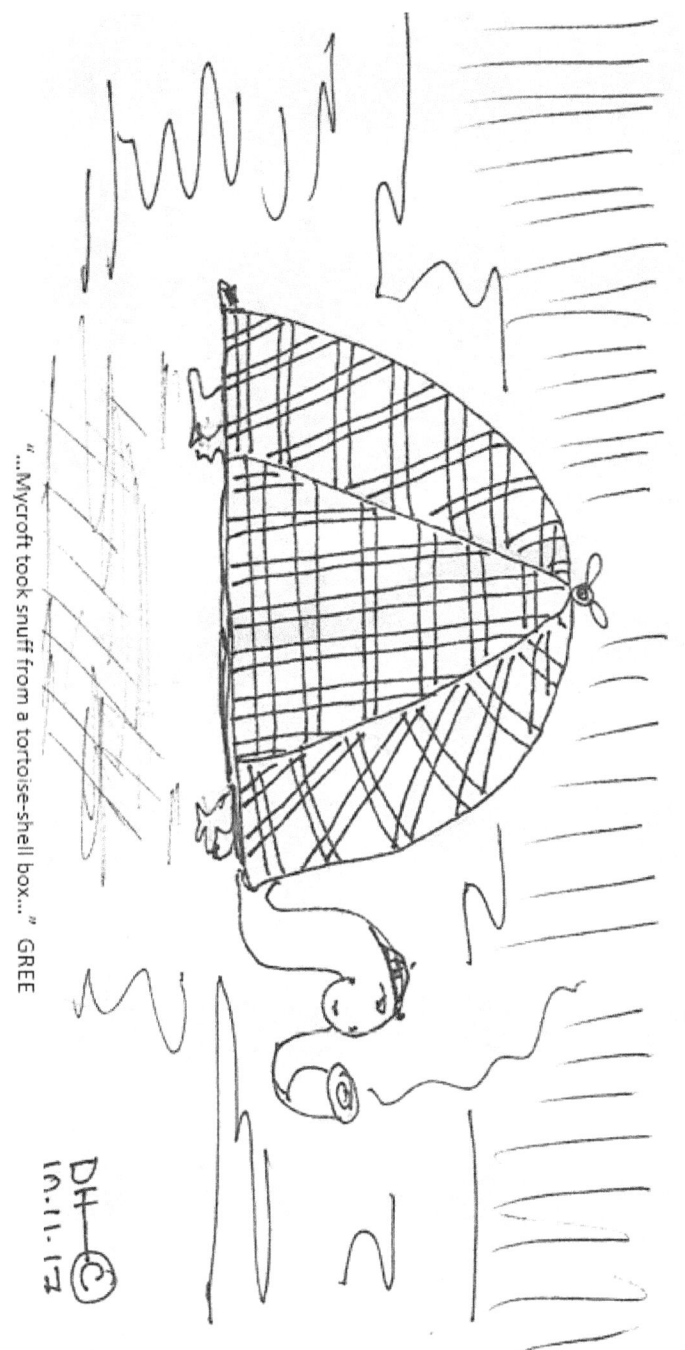

Sherlock Holmes Tortoise

"...Mycroft took snuff from a tortoise-shell box..." GREE

103

Sherlock Holmes Forever

"...while mine may remain forever..." HOUN

104

Sherlock Holmes Plays With Rubber Gloves

"...had gloves which are impregnated with disinfectants..." BLAN

DH·C
10.24.13

105

Sherlock Holmes Enjoys Folon

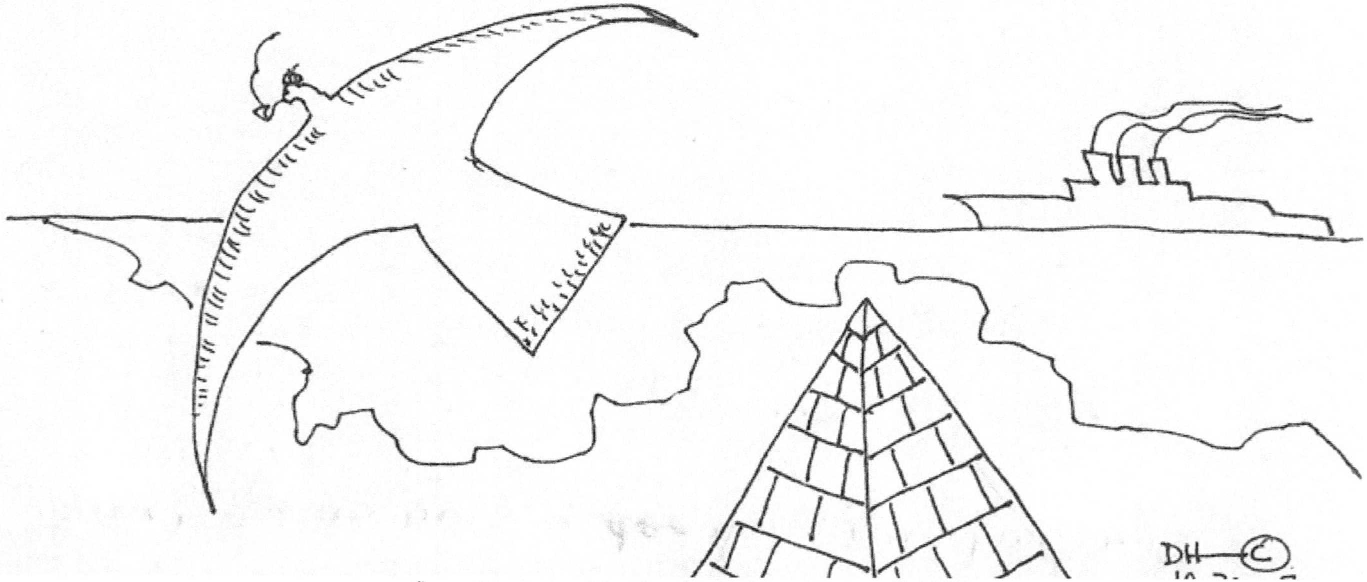

"...working as he did rather for the love of his art..." SPEC

Sherlock Holmes Gets the Boot

"...He held an old black boot in the air...." HOUN

107

Sherlock Holmes Is a Foot Short

"...a large foot or small..." GOLD

108

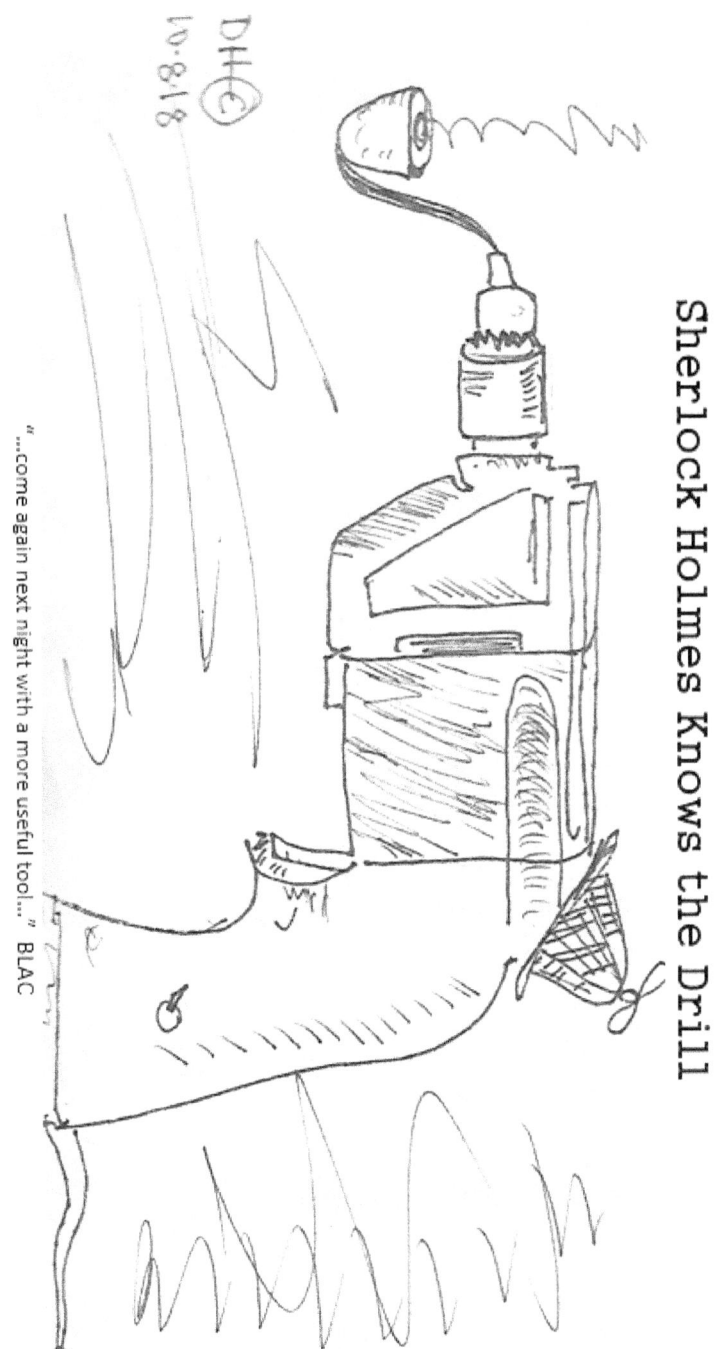

Sherlock Holmes Knows the Drill

"...come again next night with a more useful tool..." BLAC

DH©
10.8.18

Sherlock Holmes Is a Little Froggy

"...and how came it in the pond?..." MUSG

Sherlock Holmes Channels Vera Carp

"...a woman of Spanish blood..." HOUN

111

Sherlock Holmes Visits McSorley's

"...Your beer should be excellent..." BLUE

Sherlock Holmes Views the Super Blue, Full—Moon

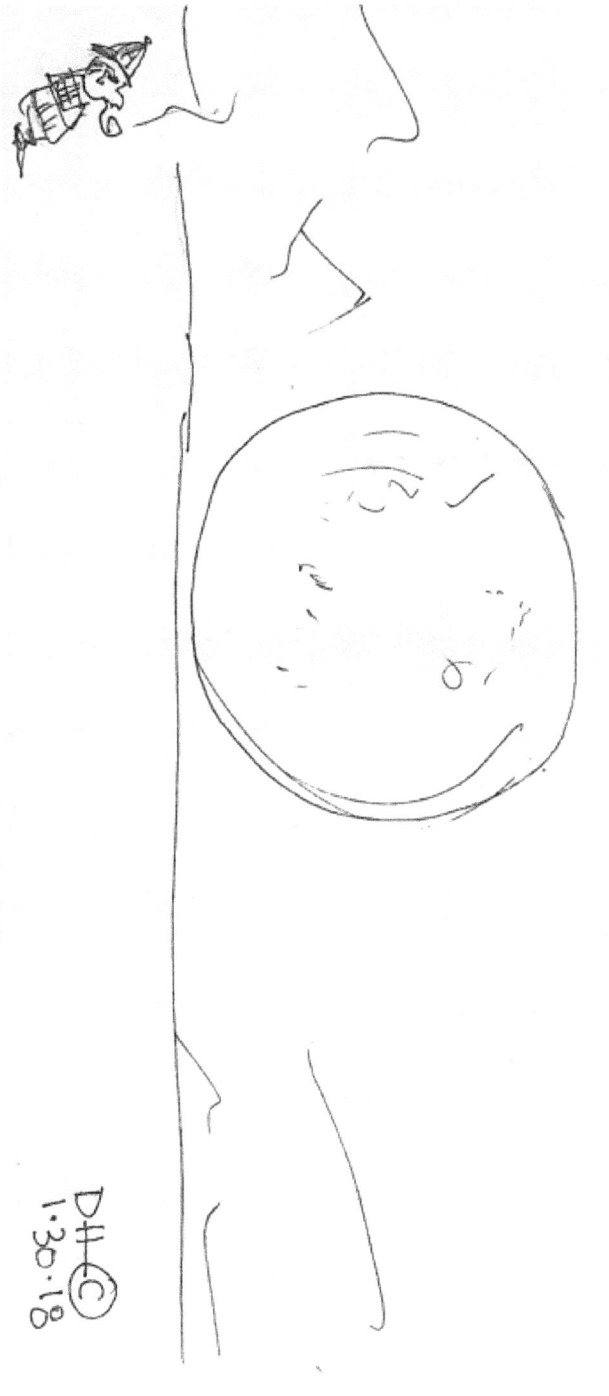

"...The moon shone clear above them..." HOUN

DH+C
1·30·18

"...like the Roman miser..." STUD

Sherlock Holmes Enjoys the Eagle's Victory

"...But you do occasionally find a carrion crow among the eagles...." SHOS

Sherlock Holmes Does a Swan Dive

"...going for a swan, I see...." LION

DH-C
2.23.18

116

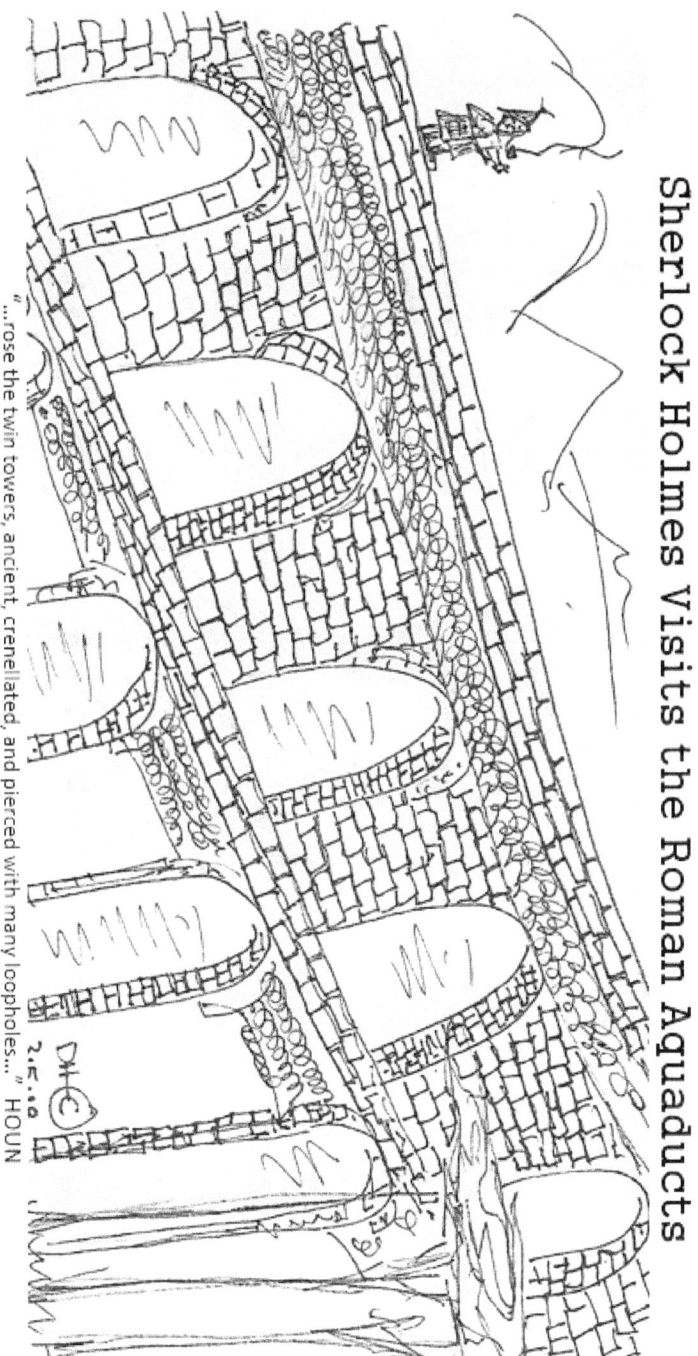

Sherlock Holmes Visits the Roman Aquaducts

"...rose the twin towers, ancient, crenellated, and pierced with many loopholes..." HOUN

Sherlock Holmes Valet of Fear

"...the valet was out for the evening..." SECO

118

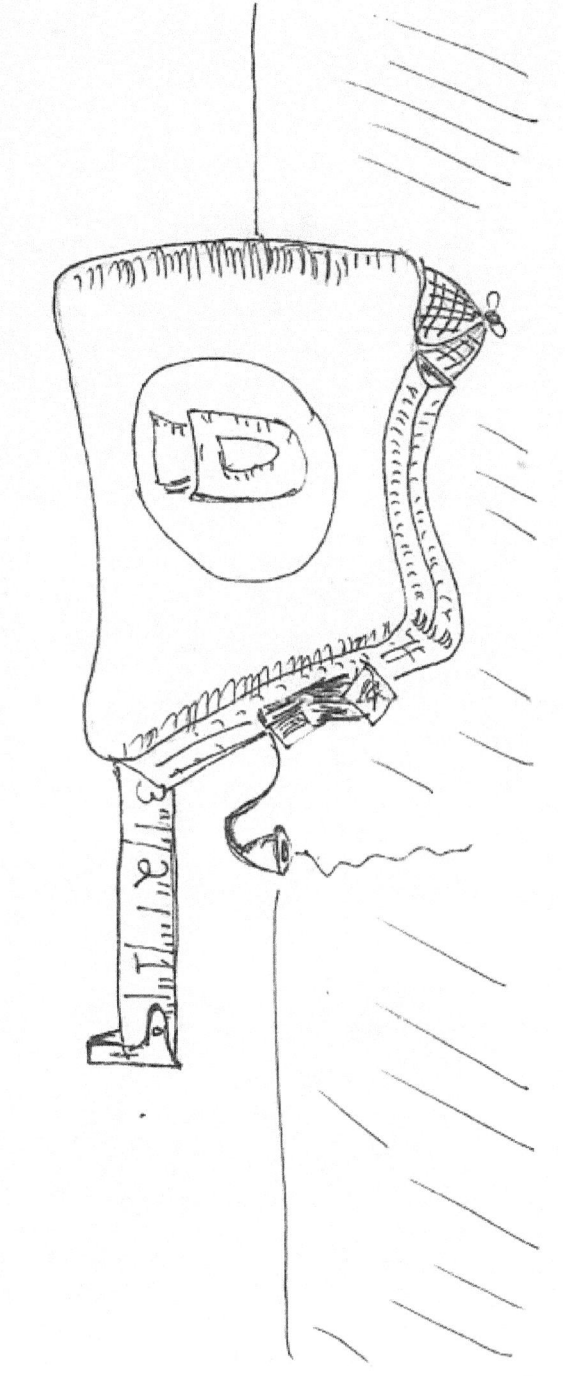

Sherlock Holmes Always Measures Up

"...he whipped out his lens and tape-measure ..." SIGN

Sherlock Holmes Listens to Horace Greeley

"...but whether north, south, east, or west, I had no idea..." ENGI

Sherlock Holmes Luck of the Irish

"...came from the north of Ireland..." CARD

DH
3.17.18

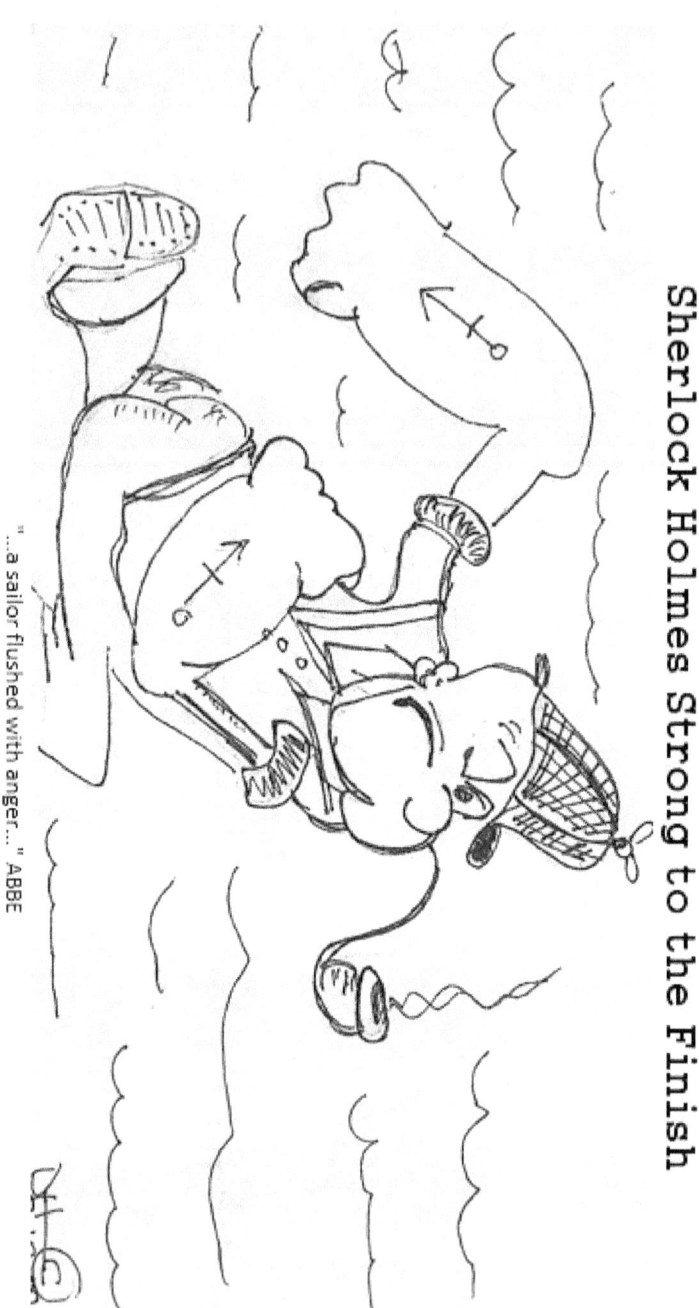

Sherlock Holmes Strong to the Finish

"...a sailor flushed with anger..." ABBE

122

Sherlock Holmes at the Warring G. Harding Memorial

"....grave enough...." REDH

Sherlock Holmes – The Long Arm of the Law

"...with far reaching consequences...." DYIN

DH-C
4.17.18

"...a long curved nose like the beak of an eagle...." MAZA

Sherlock Holmes Eats a Chopped Beef Sandwich

"...Some cold beef and a glass of beer..." SCAN

Sherlock Holmes in an Ocala, FL Sinkhole

"...Can you pick any hole in that, Mr. Holmes?..." LADY

127

Sherlock Holmes visits Manaus Brazil

"...I met my wife while gold hunting in Brazil..." THOR

DH©
2.174

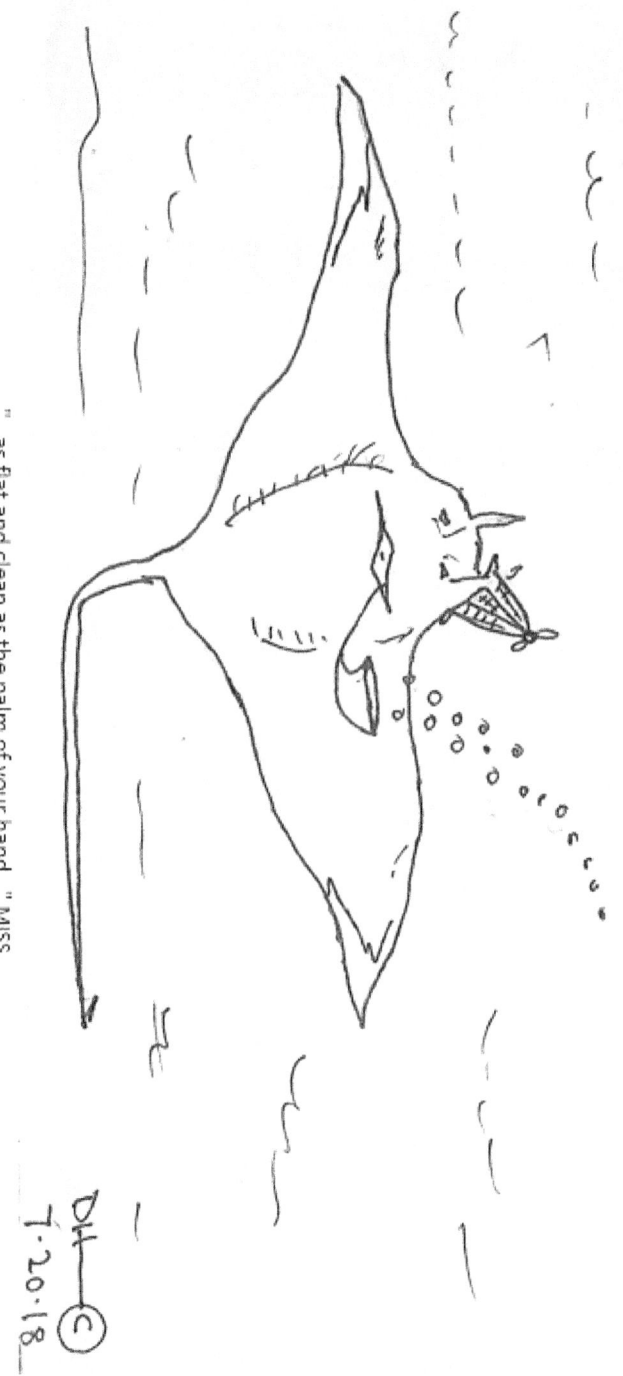

Sherlock Holmes Manta Ray

"...as flat and clean as the palm of your hand..." MISS

129

Sherlock Holmes Watches the Temperature Rise

"...the heat was far less oppressive in Croydon...." CARD

DH © 7·22·18

Sherlock Holmes Visits Atlantic City

"...born in New Jersy...." SCAN

DHC
7-22-18

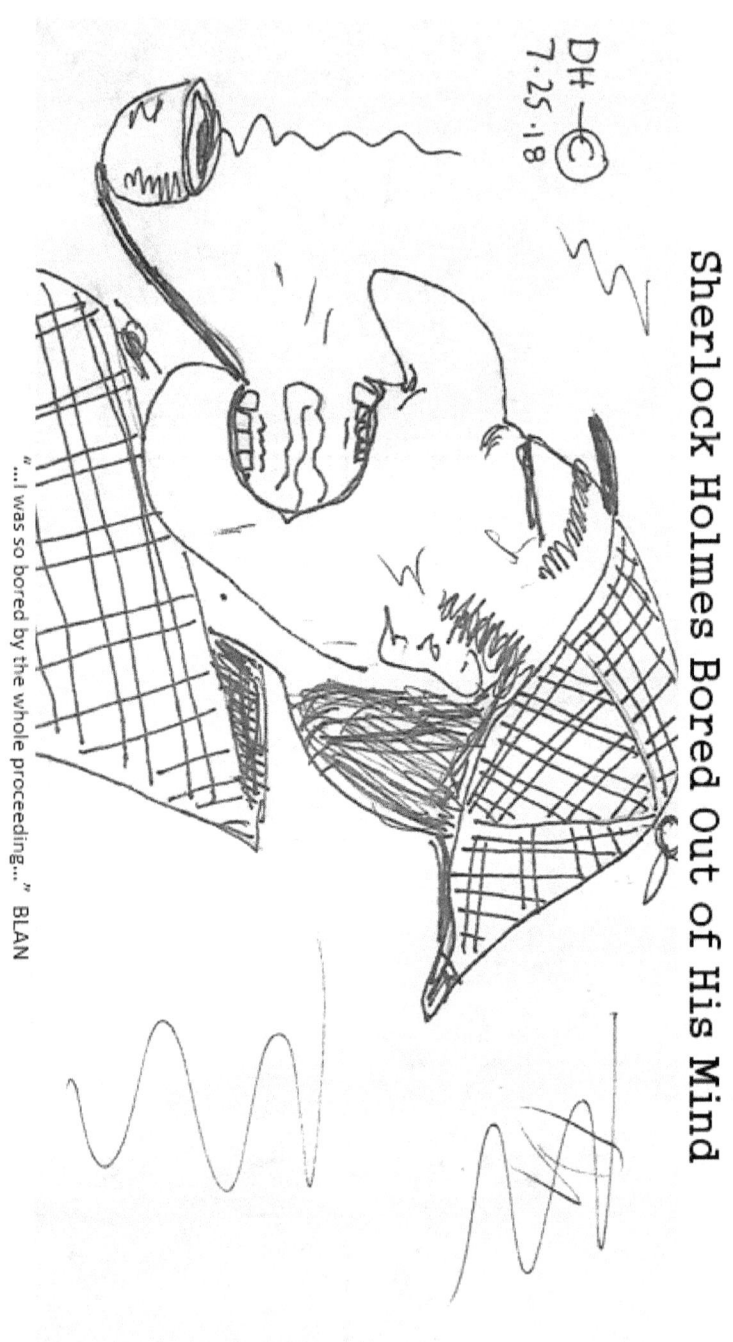

Sherlock Holmes Bored Out of His Mind

"...I was so bored by the whole proceeding..." BLAN

DH
7·25·18

Sherlock Holmes at a Disco, Again

"...a number of absurb little figures dancing across the paper..." DANC

133

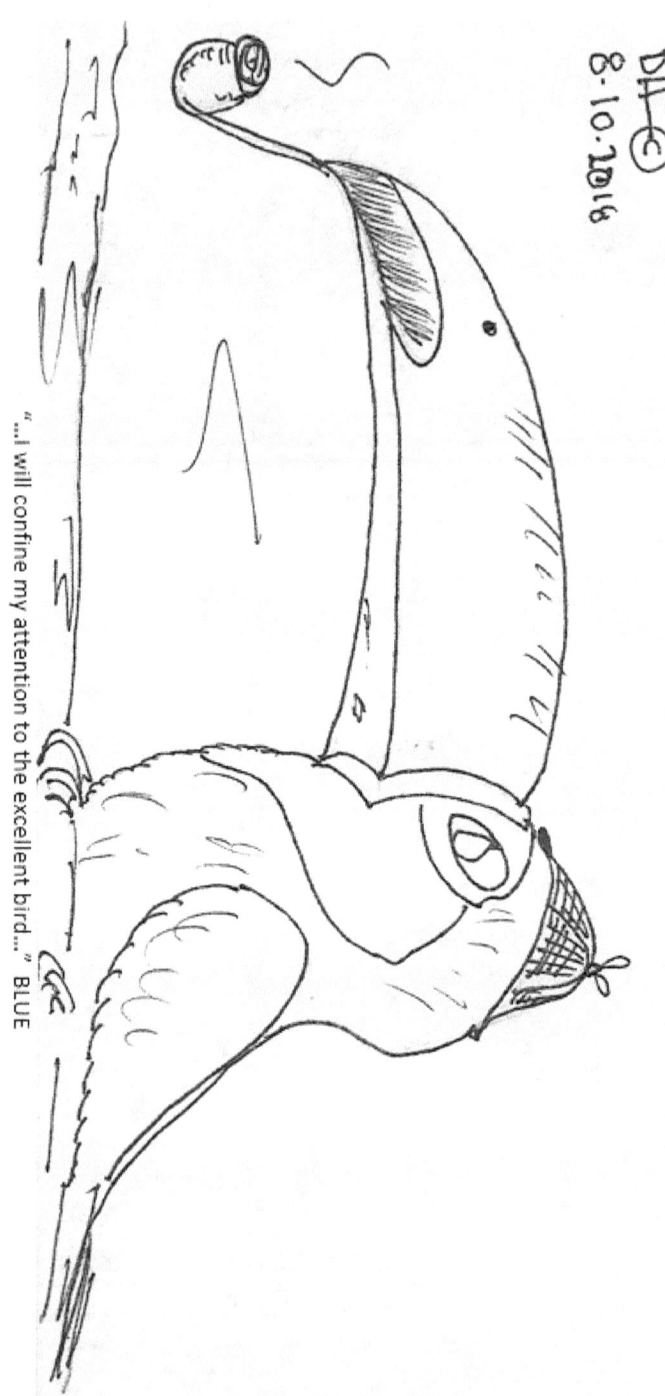

Sherlock Holmes Tucan or Not Tucan

"...I will confine my attention to the excellent bird..." BLUE

DH-C
8·10·2016

134

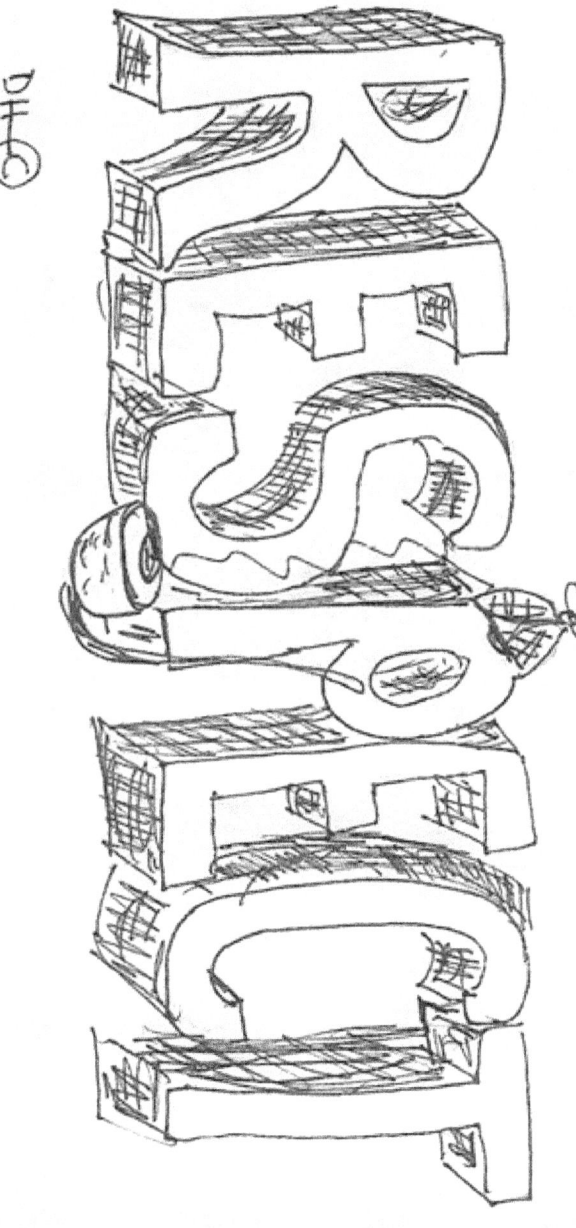

Sherlock Holmes Respects Aretha Franklin

"...I have deep respect for the extraordinary qualities of Holmes..." DYIN

Sherlock Holmes Inspects His New Toms

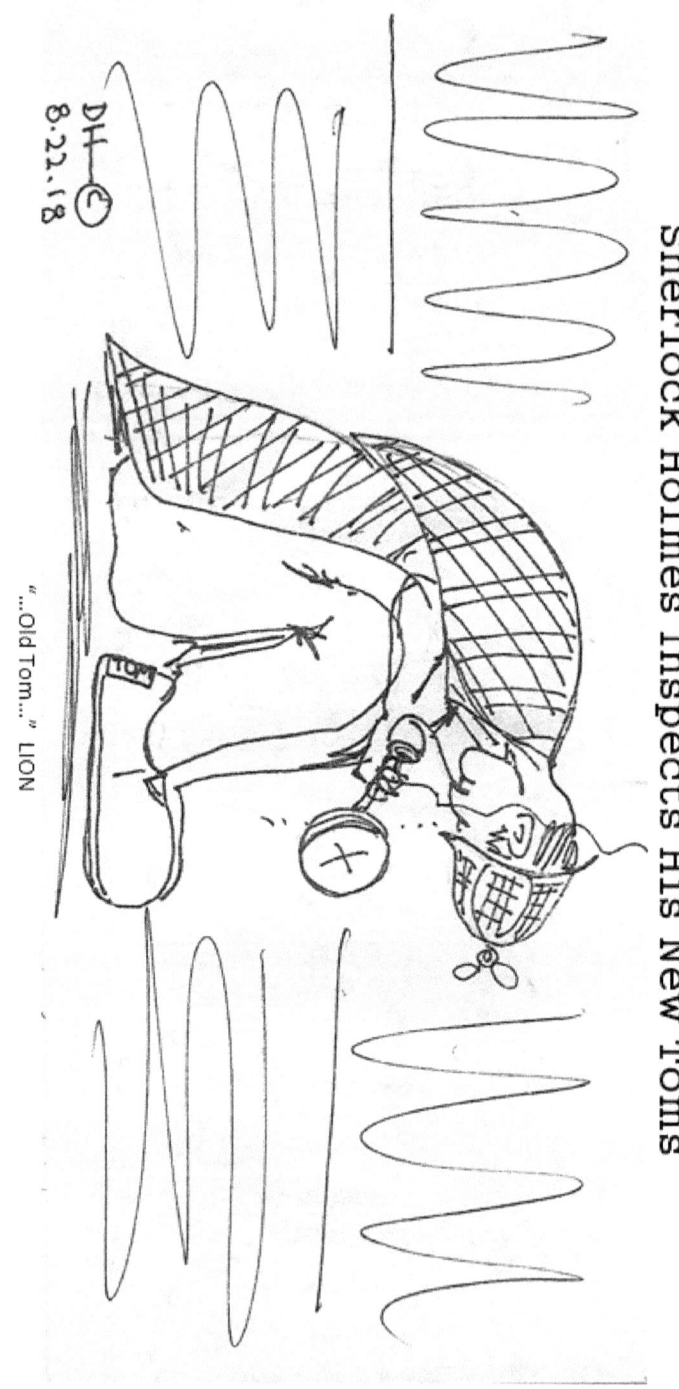

"...Old Tom..." LION

DH
8.22.18

Sherlock Holmes Chairman of the Board

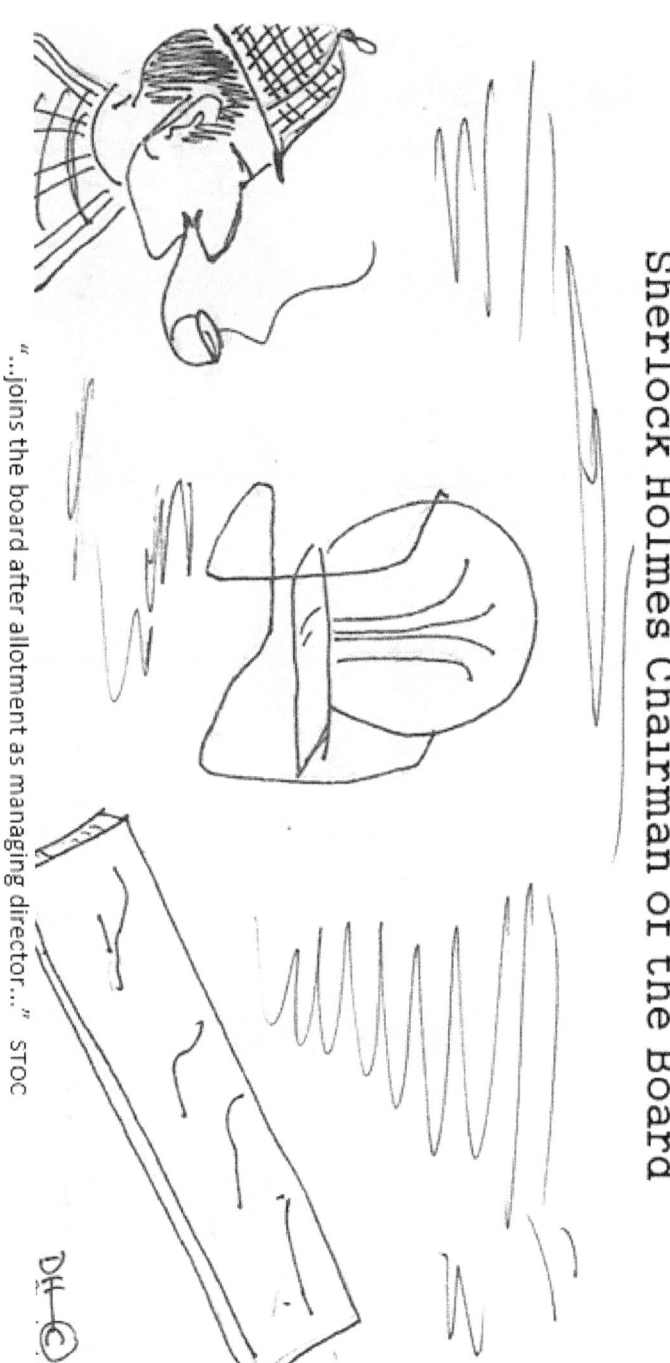

"...joins the board after allotment as managing director..." STOC

Sherlock Holmes When You Leash Expect Him

"...so I will take the liberty of fastening the leather leash..." MISS

Sherlock Holmes: Lithotomy Position

"...This he opened and made a careful examination..." BERY

DH—©
9-7-18

139

"...a man with so large a brain must have something in it..." BLUE

Sherlock Holmes Visits Sumatra

"...the giant rat of Sumatra..." SUSS

141

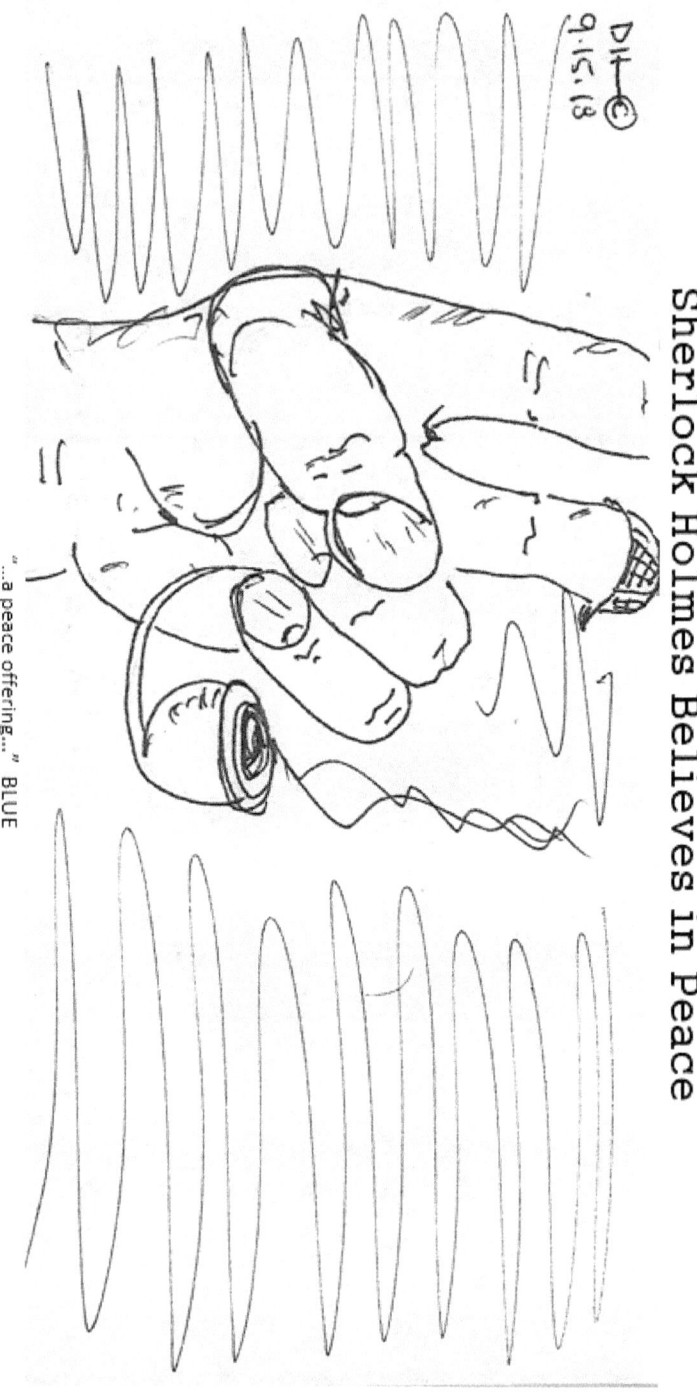

Sherlock Holmes Believes in Peace

"....a peace offering...." BLUE

DH © 9.15.13

Sherlock Holmes Money in the Bank

"...large sums of money..." BERY

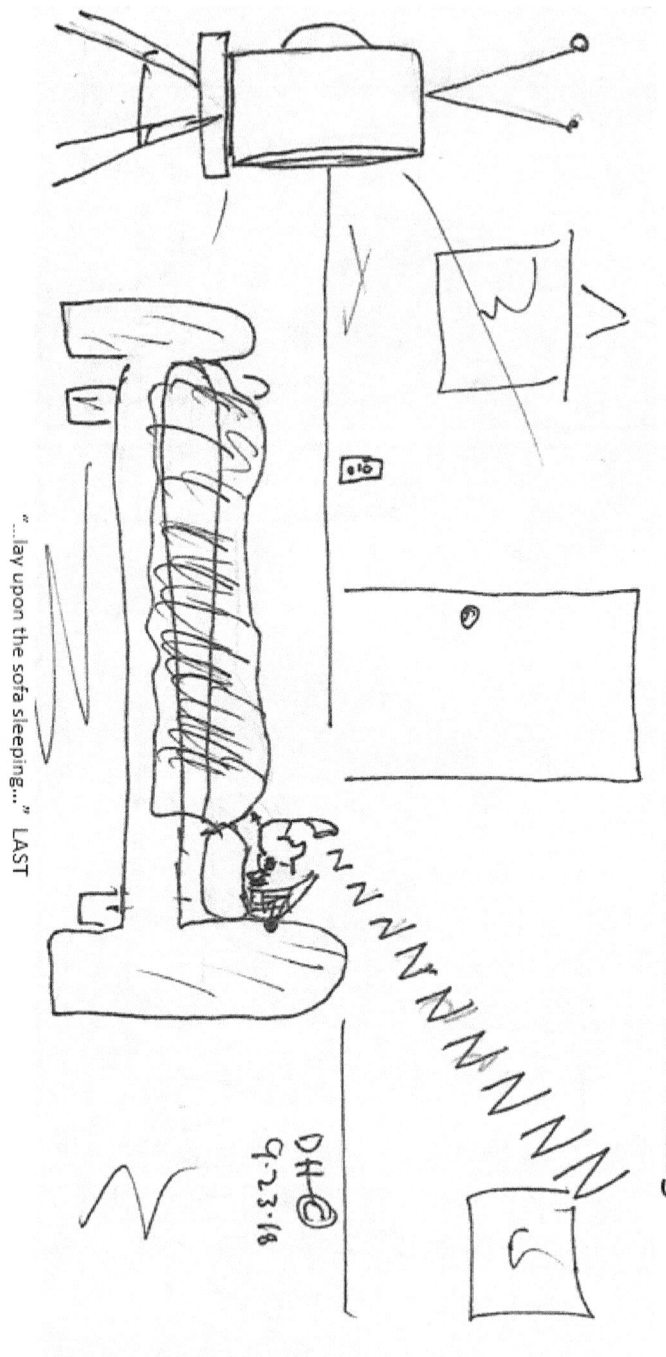

"....lay upon the sofa sleeping...." LAST

DHC©
8.23.16

Sherlock Holmes Man of Mystery

"...What is this extraordinary mystery?..." BERY

145

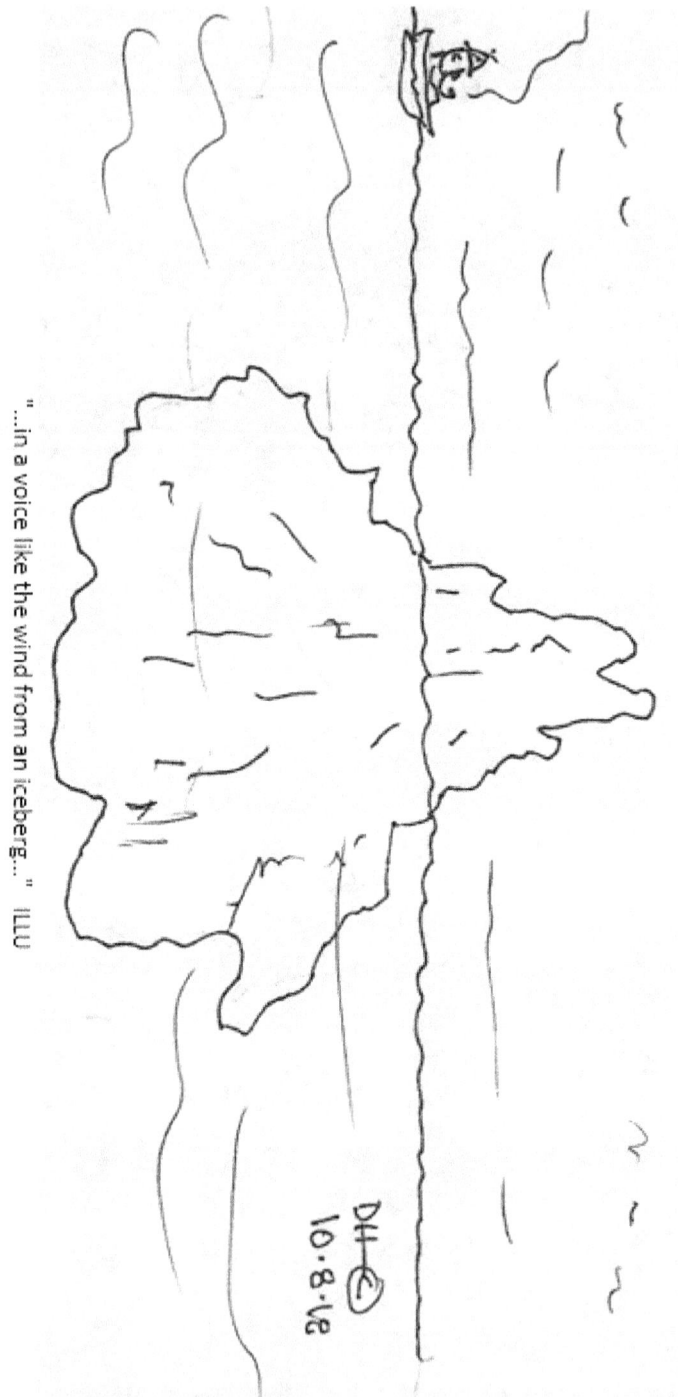

"...in a voice like the wind from an iceberg..." ILLU

Sherlock Holmes and an Iceberg

Sherlock Holmes: The Original Thinker

"...an abstract thinker..." FINA

DHC © 10.14.18

Sherlock Holmes Just Because

"...Just because they have never heard of it..." GREE

DAG
10·28·18

148

Sherlock Holmes Does the Weather

"...You like this weather?..." CHAS

149

Sherlock Holmes Accepts Everyone

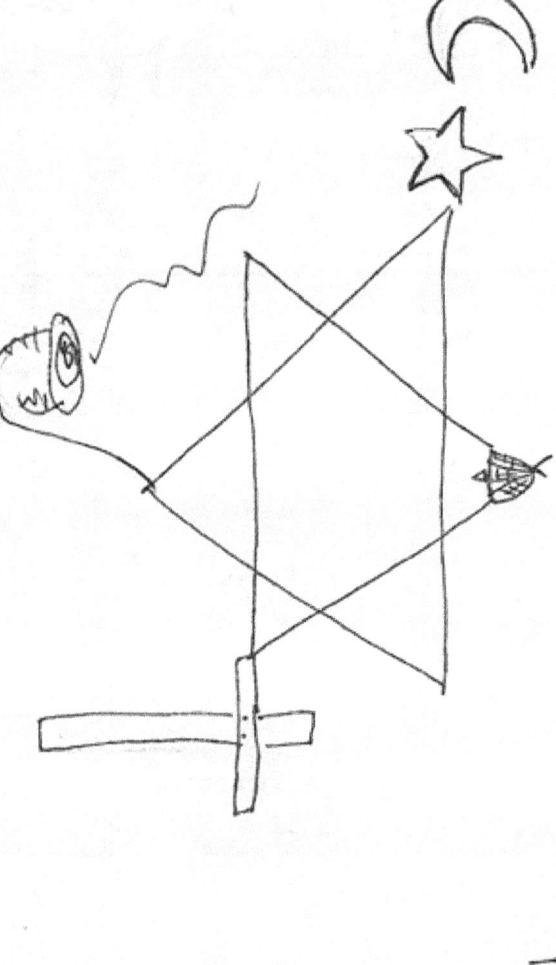

DH-© 10·31·18

"...there was something noble in the simple faith of our visitor which compelled our respect..." IDEN

Sherlock Holmes Points to a Cactus

"...He and I seemed to be the only living things between the high arch at the sky and the desert beneath...." HOUN

Sherlock Holmes Mr. Natural

"...it's natural we should take an interest..." BLAN

DH 12-25-18

Sherlock Holmes Napping

"...but Singleton was not caught napping...." STUD

Sherlock Holmes Revisits Panploma

"....He was surely not gored by a bull?...." PRIO

154

Sherlock Holmes Gets His Ducks in a Row

"...there was ecellent wild duck ..." GLOR

"...enough in his box to buy the thing right up from keel to main-truck..." GLOR

Sherlock Holmes En Guard

"...bar fencing and boxing..." GLOR

157

Sherlock Holmes Delivers Flowers

"...so I say again that we have much to hope from the flowers..." NAVA

Sherlock Holmes Flying by the Seat of His Pants

"...We were flying swiftly along...." HOUN

Sherlock Holmes Eats at Sobrino de Botin, Madrid

"...You would have soon seen a dead pig...." BLAC

160

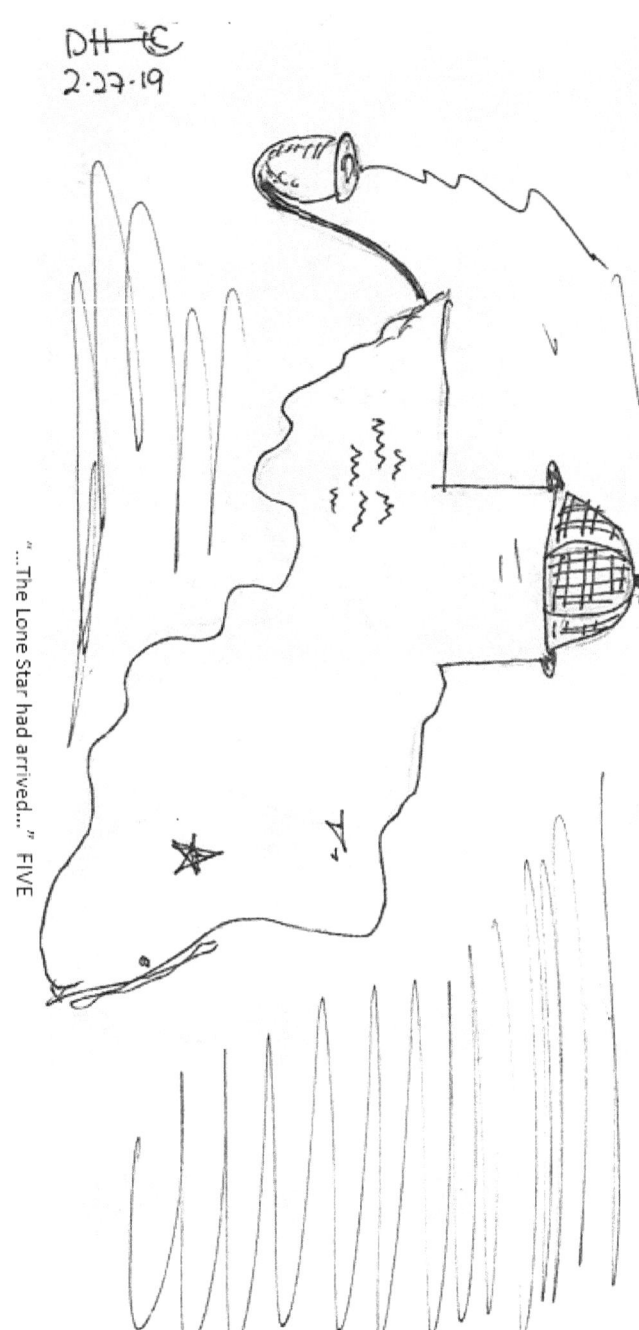

Sherlock Holmes Loves Texas

"...The Lone Star had arrived...." FIVE

Sherlock Holmes Ostrich Racer

"...hung like an immense ostrich..." ENGI

DHC
2·28·19

Sherlock Holmes Plays the Oboe While Smoking

"...a formodable instrument..." HOUN

Sherlock Holmes Enjoys the Sea—Breeze

"...but the evening has brought a breeze with it..." RESI

Titanic

DHC 3.12.19

Sherlock Holmes Visits an Aquarium

"...and is Count Sylvius one of your fish?..." MAZA

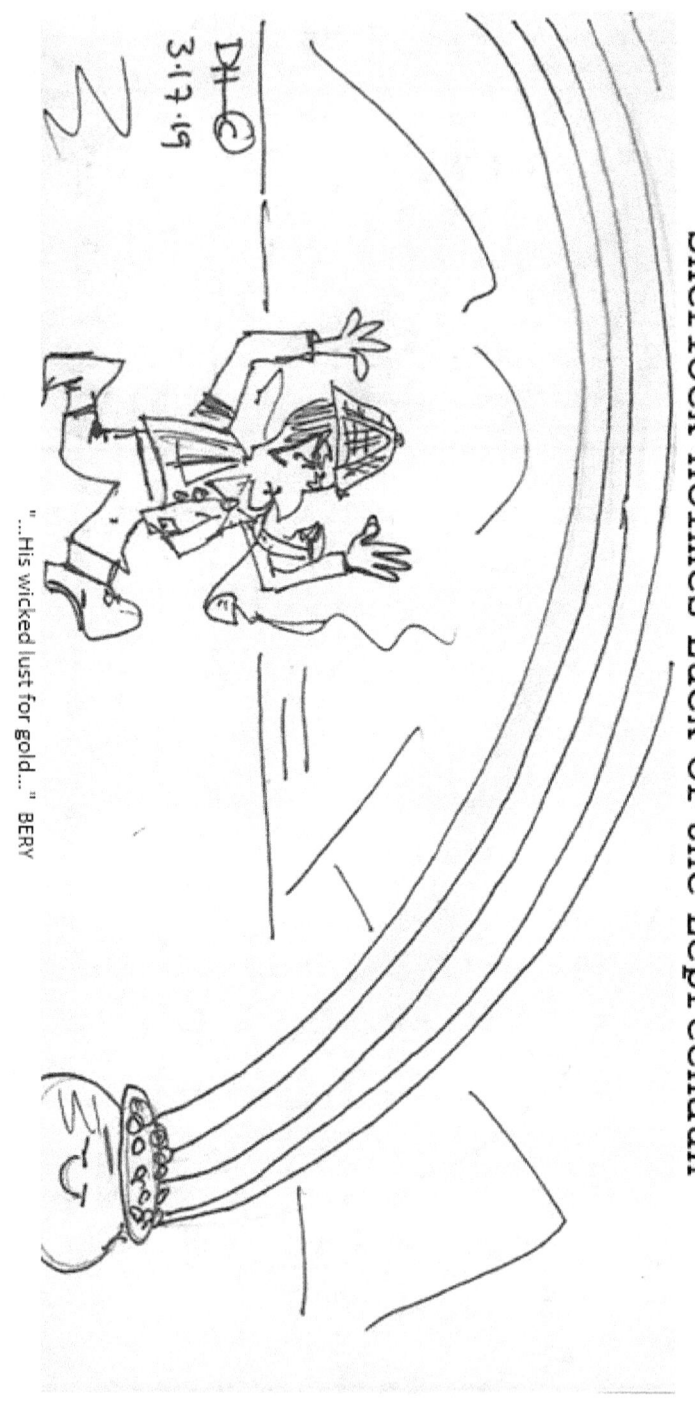

Sherlock Holmes Luck of the Leprechaun

"...His wicked lust for gold...." BERY

DH
3·17·19

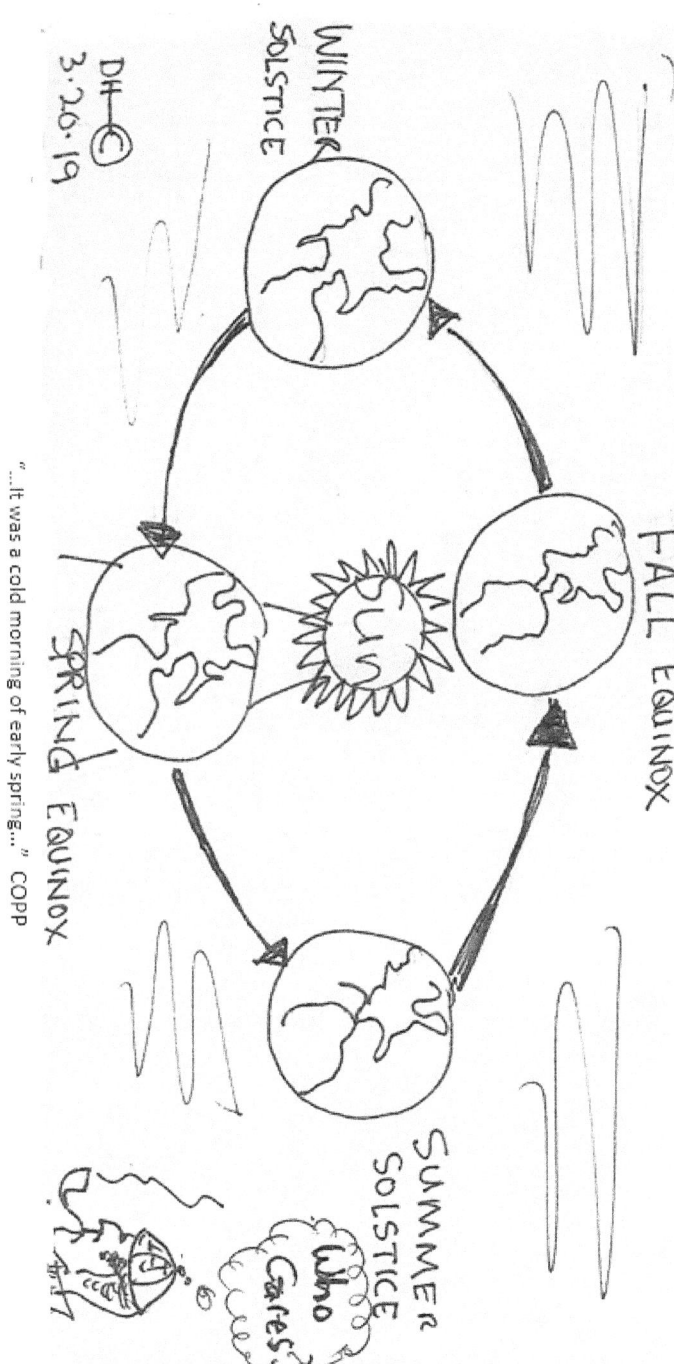

Sherlock Holmes Observes Spring Equinox

WINTER SOLSTICE

DH 3.20.19

FALL EQUINOX

SPRING EQUINOX

SUN

SUMMER SOLSTICE

Who Cares?

"...It was a cold morning of early spring..." COPP

167

Sherlock Holmes Grinning

"...Isn't it gorgeous!" said Holmes, grinning over his coffee cup..." SIGN

Sherlock Holmes Over the Edge

" ...he missed his path and walked over the edge..."   FIVE

Sherlock Holmes Rides a Jackolope

"...a twenty-mile ride which will lead you to the spot..." FIVE

Sherlock Holmes Enters the Twilight Zone

$E=mc^2$

"...Slowly the twilight crept down as the sun sank behind the high towers..." PRIO

Sherlock Holmes visits Lisbon

NOVIDADES CONFECÇÕNES

"...Holmes had been examining the window...." BLAC

" ...belle dome sans merci..." 3GAB

DHC
4·15·19

173

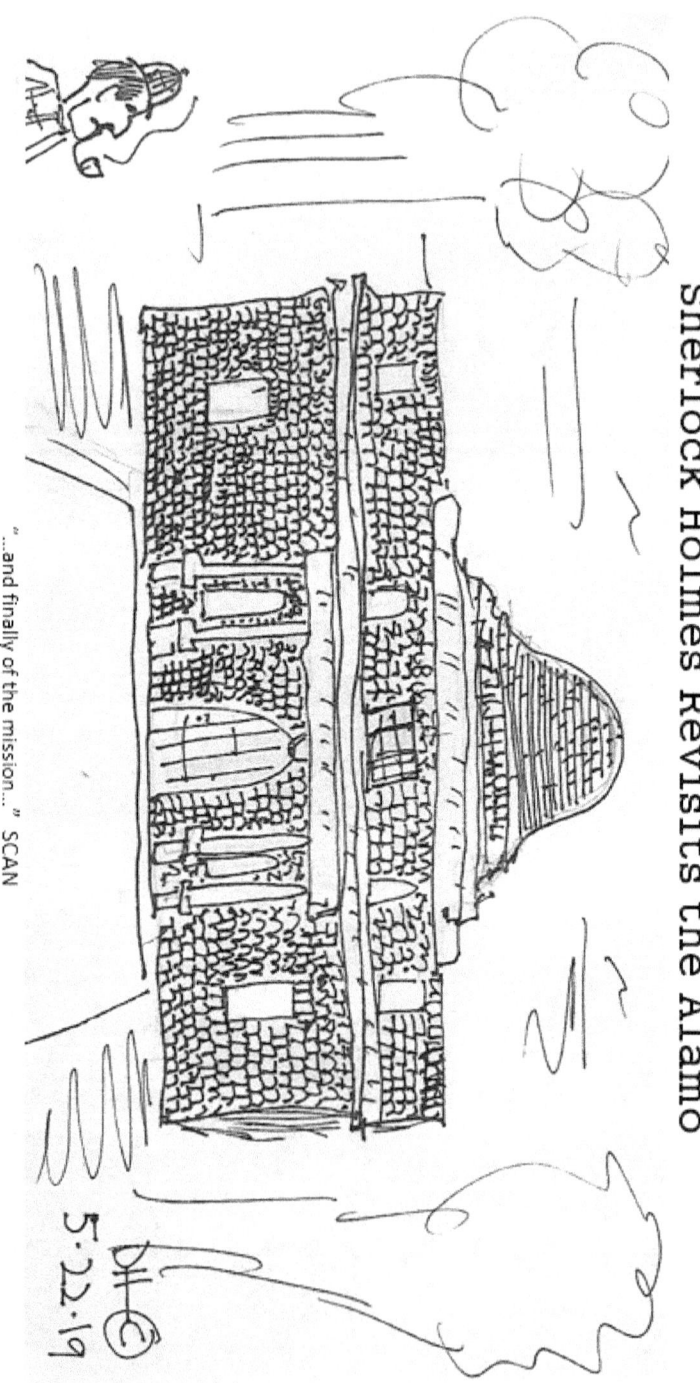

Sherlock Holmes Revisits the Alamo

"...and finally of the mission...." SCAN

5-22-19

Sherlock Holmes: A Whale of a Tale

"...one who had been a whaler..." BLAC

Sherlock Holmes Is Simply the Best!

"...and perhaps, after all, it is for the best..." SPEC

176

Sherlock Holmes Love Play—Off Hockey

"...it was frozen over..." ABBE

Sherlock Holmes Ahead of His Time

"....throwing in a question from time to time...." CARD

178

Sherlock Holmes at a Snail's Pace

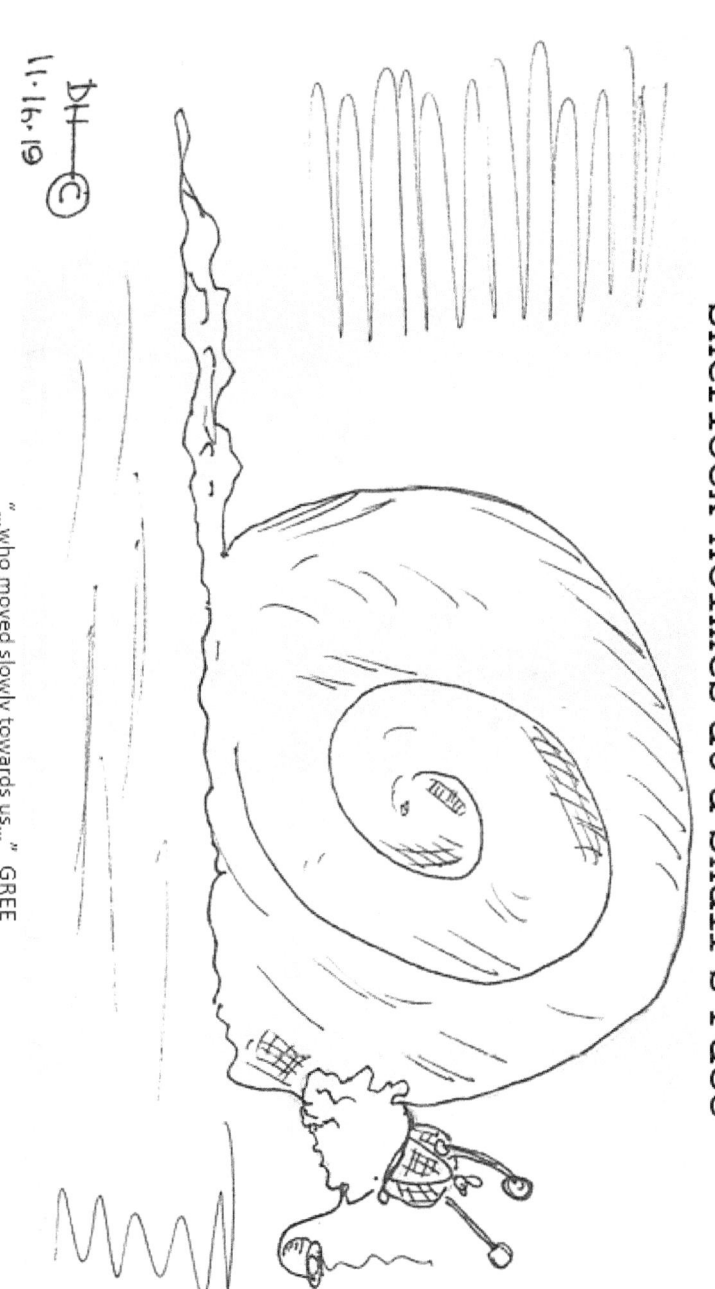

"...who moved slowly towards us..." GREE

179

Sherlock Holmes Mourns the Death of Democracy

"...even he mourned darkly..." VALL

2.5.20

180

Sherlock Holmes Flies to Atlanta

"...That is John Hebron, of Atlanta..." YELL

DH
9-10-20

Sherlock Holmes Plays Hockey in a Bubble

"...My heart bubbling over with thankfulness and joy..." HOUN

* Not bald, just where the hat belongs

"...he would look up and measure with a glance the distancing which separated..." SIGN

Sherlock Holmes at Peace with Himself

"...peace of mind..." HOUN

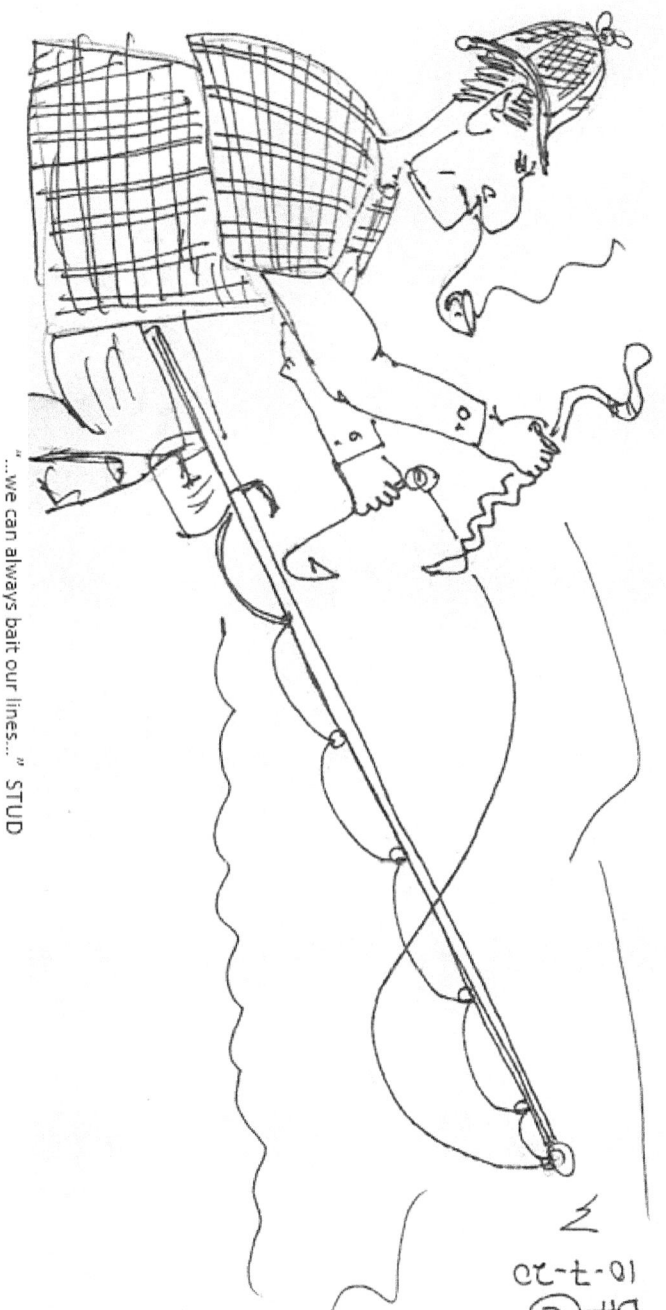

Sherlock Holmes Master-Baiter

"...we can always bait our lines..." STUD

Sherlock Holmes Attends the V. P. Debate

"...that was the subject of the debate..." VALL

DH-C
10.9.2020

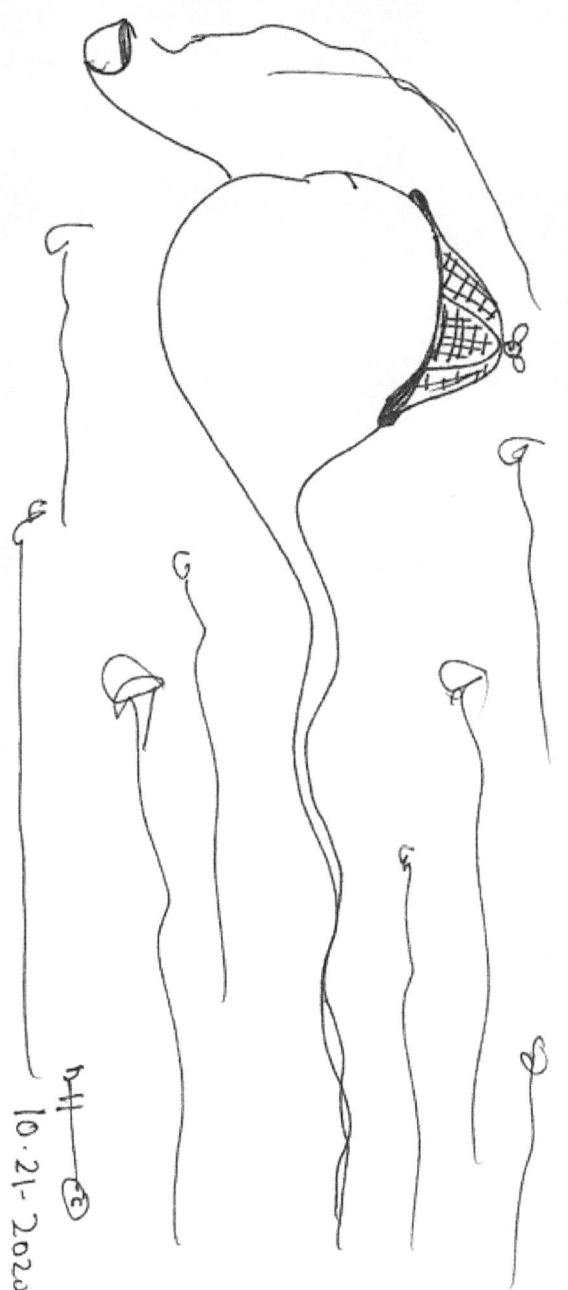

Sherlock Holmes Happy Sperm

"...and yet kept swimminh for a surpising time..." GLOR

10-21-2020

Sherlock Holmes Gets His Shit Together

"....a particular maloderous product...." DANC

Sherlock Holmes Oders Chicken Fingers

"...like some huge awkward chicken, torn squawking from its coop...." 3GAB

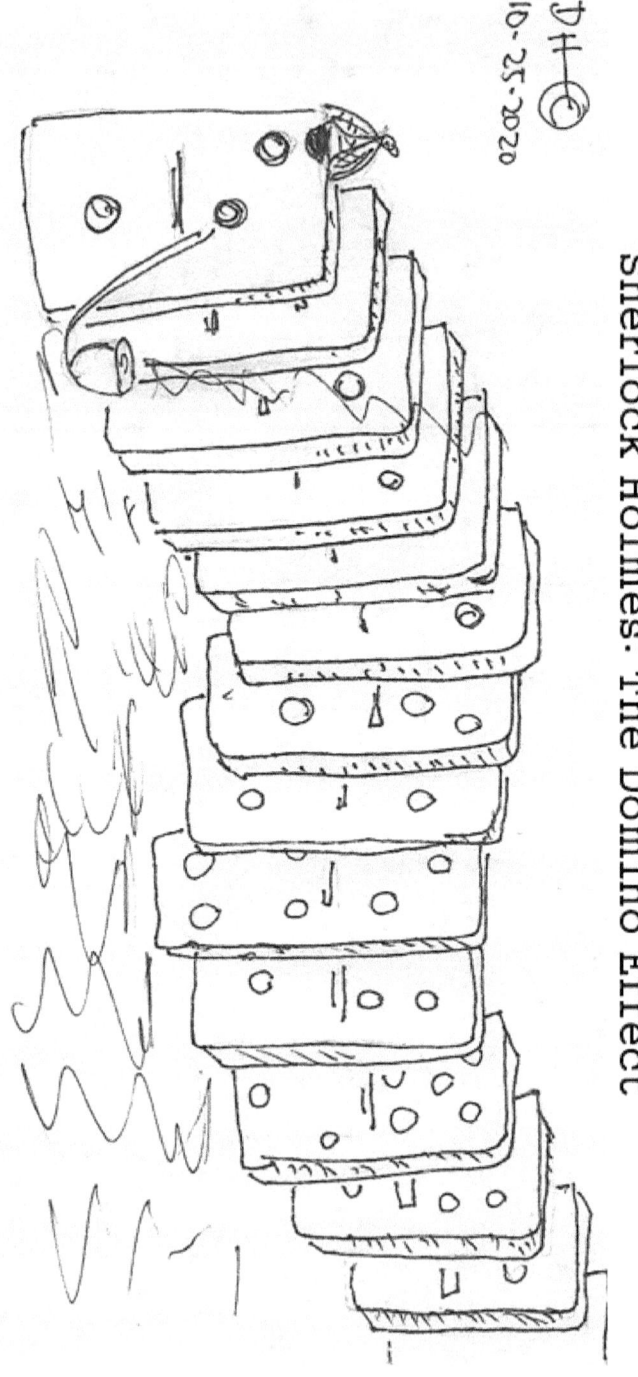

"...it may well have been cause and effect..." FIVE

Sherlock Holmes' Real Fine 409

"...would do inside which some powerful engine was at work..." STUD

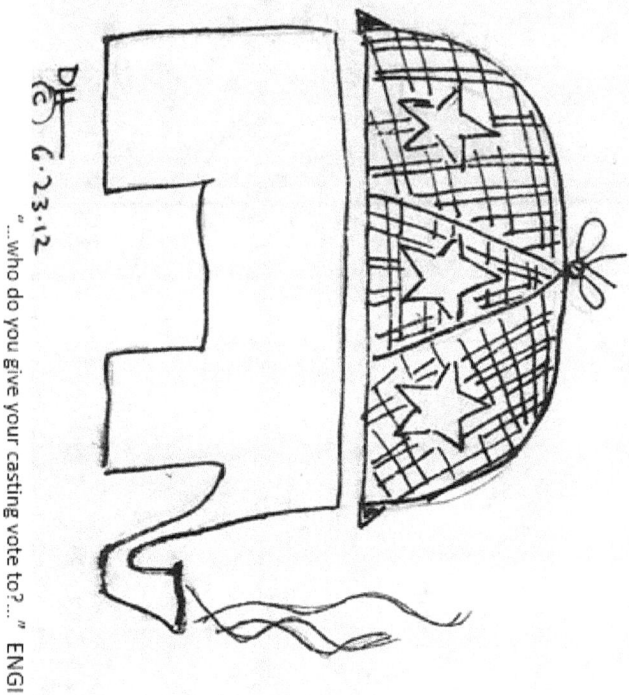

"...who do you give your casting vote to?..." ENGI

DH
© 6.23.12

Sherlock Holmes Never Votes Democratic

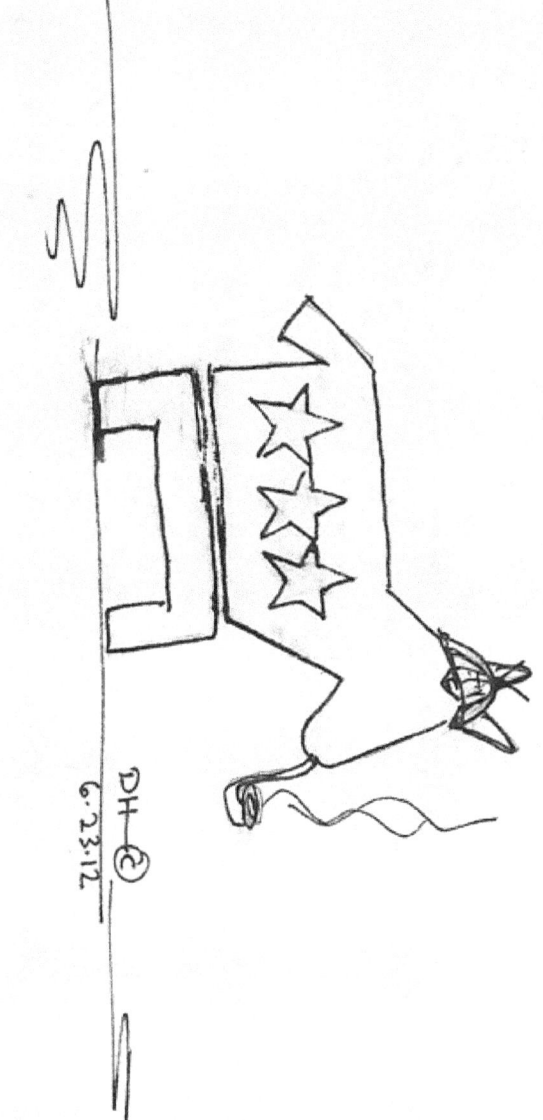

"...but I guess that in New York this lady's husband will receive a pretty general vote of thanks..." REDC

193

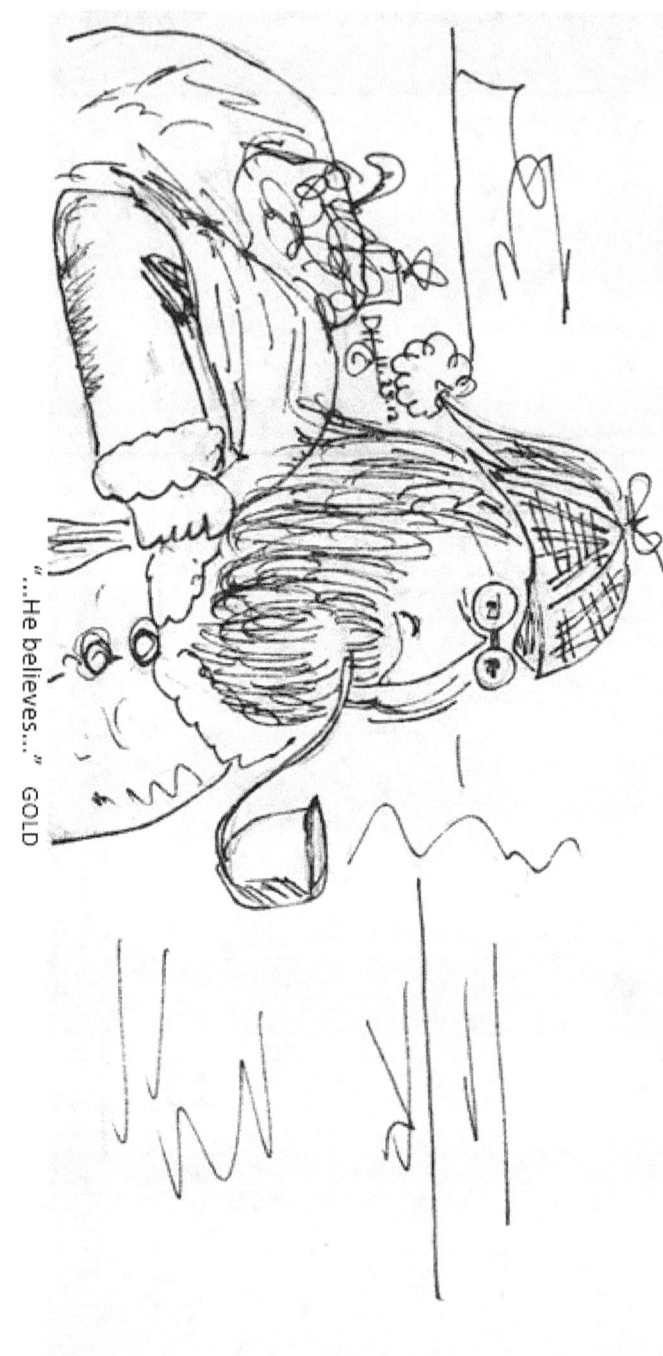

"...He believes..." GOLD

Sherlock Holmes Believes in Santa

194

Sherlock Holmes Out of Sorts

"...Well, it takes all sorts..."   GOLD

"...he was a reporter..." VALL

DHC
11-10-2024

Sherlock Holmes watches the Simpsons

"...ah, here is Simpson to report..." CROO

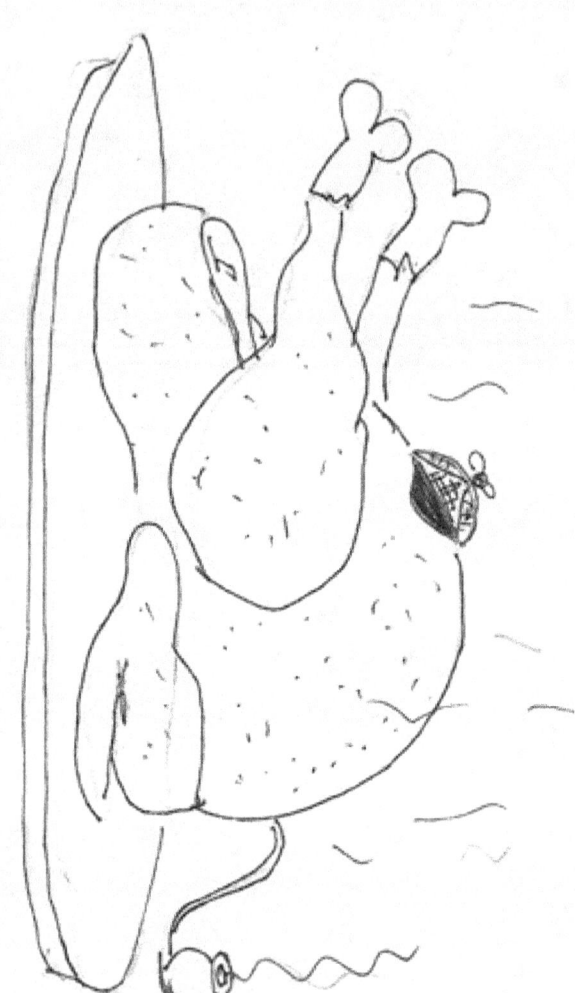

"...Turkey which called for immediate action..." BLAN

Sherlock Holmes Loves Snoopy

"...something between a beagle and a foxhound..."   MISS

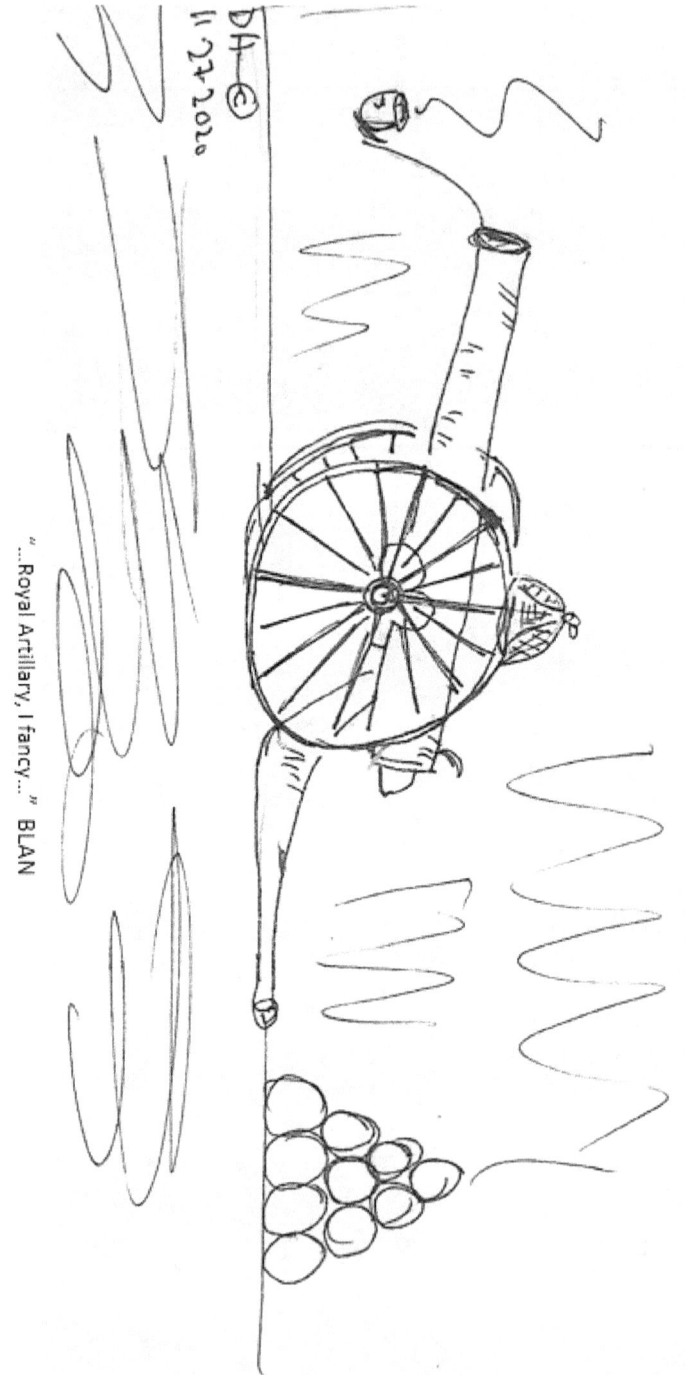

Sherlock Holmes Canon (sic)

"...Royal Artillary, I fancy..." BLAN

200

Sherlock Holmes Gets Down and Dirty

"...unkempt and dirty..." VALL

Sherlock Holmes Stuck in a Nor'Eastern

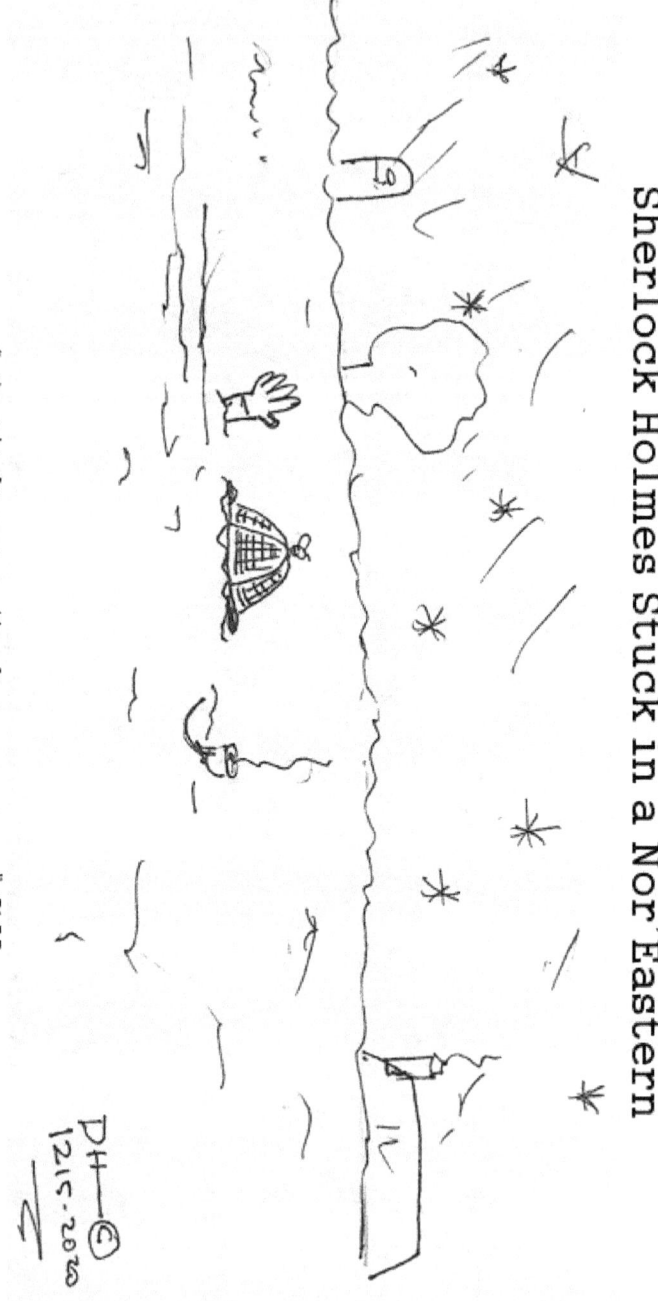

"...the sight of it was to me like a fire in a snow storm..." GLOR

202

"...I told him of the Chinese in the East End..." DYIN

Sherlock Holmes: Run Sherlock, Run

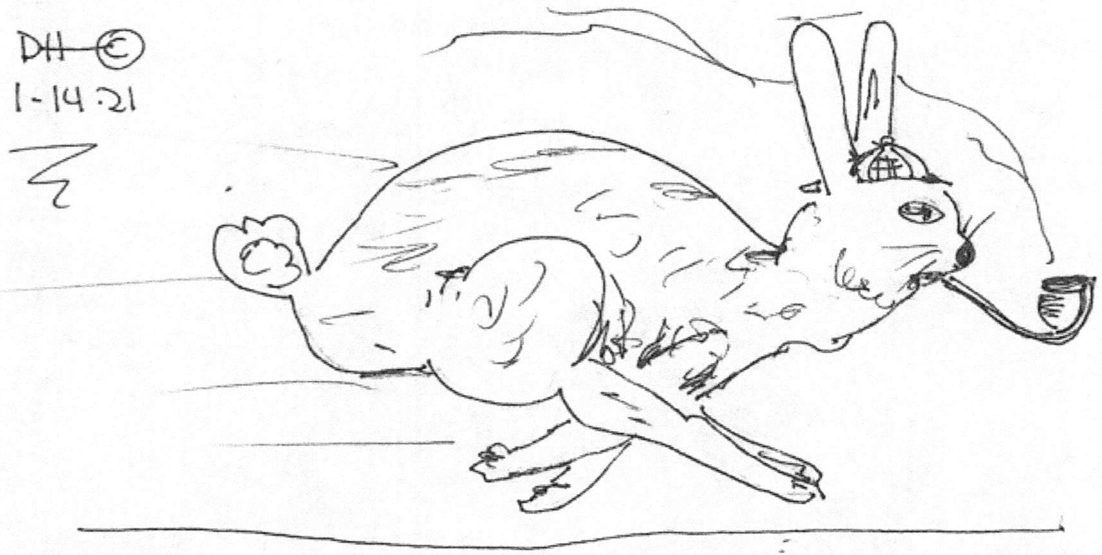

"...like a rabbit out of its burrow..." EMPT

Sherlock Holmes Has a Spot of Tea

"...it came just as we were finishing our tea ..." YELL

Sherlock Holmes Ice—Skating

DH©
1·19·21

"...Lady with a black boa at Prince's Skating Club..." REDC

Sherlock Holmes and the Full Moon

"...and the moon was full..." PRIO

Sherlock Holmes Celebrates the First Goal – 2021 NHL

"....was really an object of interest to the celebrated, Mr. Sherlock Holmes...." SCAN

Sherlock Holmes The 7% Vaccination

"...a seven-per-cent. solution. Would you care to try it?..." SIGN

Sherlock Holmes Looks Twisted

"...must not be permitted to warp our judgement..." ABBE

DH
2-01-2024
©

Sherlock Holmes Re-Watches Six-Feet Under

"...It was the remark of the undertaker's wife..." LADY

"...and give me a few clear answers..." SUSS

Sherlock Holmes at the Big Game

"...is the game worth it?..." ILLU

DHC©
2.7.2021

"....No he was flying...." SIGN

214

Sherlock Holmes Keeps on Truckin'

"...long lines of trucks piled with coal and iron ore..." VALL

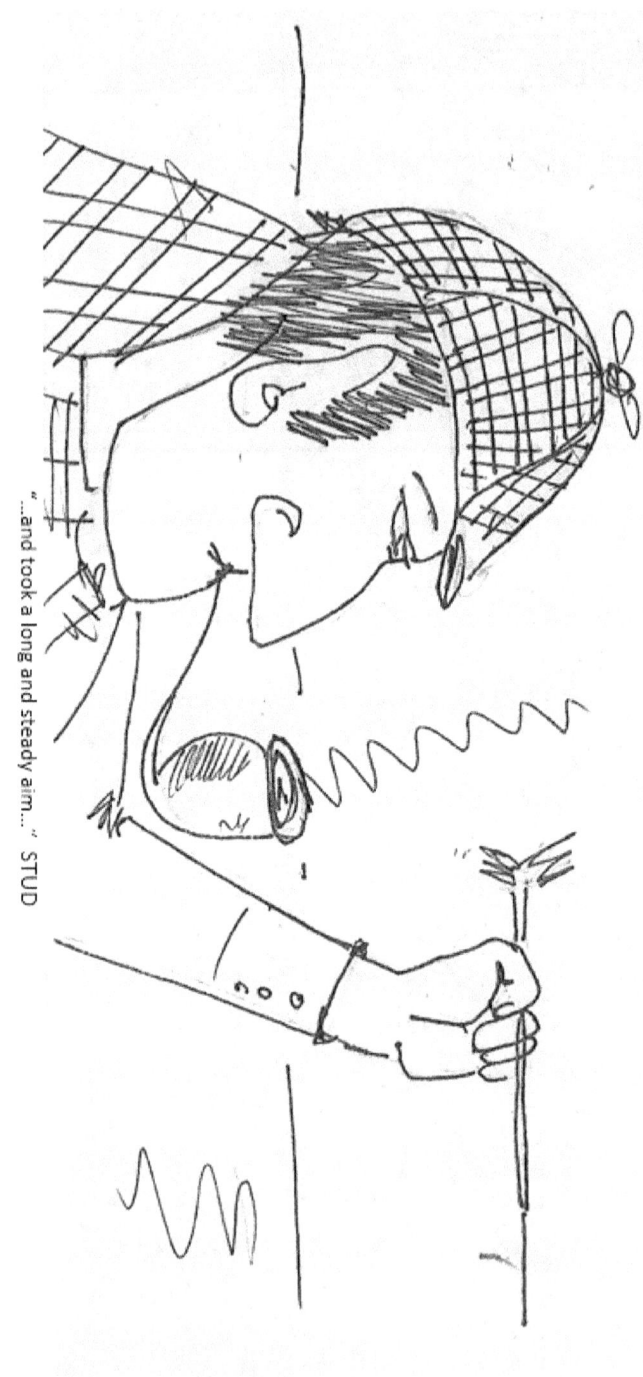

Sherlock Holmes Takes Aim

"...and took a long and steady aim..." STUD

Sherlock Holmes Is All Tied Up

"...But surely his hand was not tied up like that yesterday..." NAVA

Sherlock Holmes Looms Large

"...in Baker Street to see the loom of the opposite houses..."   BRUC

Sherlock Holmes Visits Montepulciano

"...there was a bottle of wine on the side board...." ABBE

Sherlock Holmes Loves His Wine

"...it's a good wine, Holmes..." LAST

Sherlock Holmes Visits Kitty Hawk, NC

4·10·21

"...as keen as on that memorable flight..." STUD